MINIONS OF THE TIGER

By
CHESTER S. GEIER

I0541455

ARMCHAIR FICTION
PO Box 4369, Medford, Oregon 97504

*For more information about Armchair Books and products, visit our
website at...*

www.armchairfiction.com

Or email us at...

armchairfiction@yahoo.com

A MAD SCIENTIST'S DEADLY GAME

Chester S. Geier will never be remembered as an upper tier writer of science fiction and fantasy. That mantle falls on the shoulders of Asimov, Bradbury, Heinlein and others. But there's no doubt that Geier knew how to tell a good, entertaining story. "Minions of the Tiger" is one such tale. It's well-written and chock full of supernatural peril and action-filled situations. It's obvious that Geier was a big fan of Universal horror movies of the 1940s, because "Minions of the Tiger's" storyline is much in the vein of films like "Night Monster" and "The Mad Ghoul." While you're reading along it's easy to imagine Bela Lugosi as the mad Hindu scientist and Evelyn Ankers as the lady in distress, all set to a Hans J. Salter music score flowing along in the background. No...Geier will never be remembered as one of the greats, but "Minions of the Tiger" is clear evidence of his prowess as a first-rate storyteller.

For a complete 2nd novel turn to page 139

CAST OF CHARACTERS

JEFFREY CORBIN
He was a young lawyer, and a pretty good one, too. But his latest case would take him into realms where no laws prevailed.

DORIS MELHORN
Unspoiled by her wealth and grounded in common sense, she seemed to have a natural aversion to Amkeddar—at least initially.

DR. SUBHAS AMKEDDAR
He was suave and personable when he so desired, but this strange doctor from India was the personification of living evil.

BARTON MELHORN
This wealthy businessman sensed a horrible change in his daughter, but the depth of that change staggered his imagination.

KUMARA
Strange and mysterious, she had arrived in America from India. Would her love for a madman prove to be her undoing?

DR. LORRIMER
This no-nonsense doctor knew it was impossible for a man to transform into an animal—at least that's what he thought.

CHONDHAS
Tall, dark, and strong, he was fiercely loyal to his master—and willing to commit murder for him if so ordered!

MRS. CASTLETON
This aging socialite was affable, witty, and charming—yet there seemed to be a queer strangeness evolving deep inside her.

MINIONS OF THE TIGER

MINIONS OF THE TIGER

Artwork by Henry Sharp

CHAPTER ONE
An Introduction

THE gate was locked, the headlights showed. Corbin nosed his roadster close to the ornate iron grille-work and drew to a stop. Leaning forward, he squinted through the headlight glare and into the velvety darkness beyond.

At the upper end of the driveway, through the branches of intervening trees, the lights of a house gleamed.

There were enough lights to suggest that a party was going on, but Corbin wasn't entirely certain that he had reached his destination. Though Barton Melhorn had given explicit directions over the phone for finding the Castleton mansion, Corbin excused his hesitancy on the basis that he was as yet unfamiliar with Sylvan Heights, especially with the location of the homes of its various residents.

Beyond the gate, to the left of the driveway, was a small cottage, one of its lighted windows partly visible from where

Corbin sat in the car. He decided it was the home of the caretaker, watchman, or whoever else it was that performed the ceremony of opening and closing the gate. The man would help to dispel his uncertainty. He pressed the car horn and sat back to await results.

Presently, he heard the sound of a door opening. Feet scraped on gravel. An elderly man in overalls moved into sight. He peered with narrowed eyes through the headlights, at Corbin.

"What do you want?"

"Is this the Castleton residence?" Corbin asked.

"That's right." The man narrowed his eyes a bit more. "What's your business, mister?"

Corbin felt a growing irritation. His plans for the day had gone awry enough, and the gatekeeper's suspicious nature wasn't helping matters any. He answered with a sharpness unusual for him.

"I'm supposed to be a guest at the party Mrs. Castleton is throwing. It just happens that I'm late."

The gatekeeper didn't seem to be impressed. "What's your name?"

"Corbin. Jeffrey Corbin. And now, by heaven, are you going to let me in, or do I still have to show you the birthmark on my right shoulder blade?"

"Guess it'll be all right," the gatekeeper said evenly. "Mrs. Castleton phoned me to expect a guy by the name of Corbin." He moved to the middle of the gate. A clicking sound followed, and shortly the barrier swung open.

CORBIN'S urge was to roar through, giving full vent to his annoyance, but the gatekeeper's conduct puzzled him. There was a hint of mystery about it that Corbin could not by nature ignore. And his profession was one in which inquisitiveness paid dividends.

He controlled his first impulse, moving the roadster only far enough to reach the gatekeeper's side. "Say, is there anything wrong? Or is it just that you've been seeing too many movies?"

"I don't know what you're talking about."

Corbin said patiently, "What I want to know it why you were asking all those questions a moment ago, if Mrs. Castleton phoned you to expect me. Is that a regular habit of yours, or is there anything going on?"

The gatekeeper shifted his feet, glancing up the driveway, at the house. "Well, funny things have been happening in Sylvan Heights lately. Mighty funny things."

"What sort of things?" Corbin asked.

The lines of the gatekeeper's leathery face tightened secretively. "You'll find out if you stay here long enough."

"You might drop a hint," Corbin prompted.

"All right, but I ain't going to say no more." The man leaned toward the car. "Folks in Sylvan Heights have seen tigers pussy-footing around late at night. Yes, tigers. Not harming anybody, you understand. But you can never tell what might happen."

Corbin grinned. "Interesting. But it should have been perfectly obvious to you a while ago that I wasn't a tiger."

The gatekeeper moved his bony shoulders uneasily. "Can't be too sure about that. Nope, can't be too sure at all."

Corbin stared for a moment, then fought a sudden urge to laugh. Sylvan Heights, an exclusive residential suburb inhabited by people who where as respectable as they were financially affluent, seemed the last place in the world where one would expect tigers to roam. Especially tigers that looked human and drove automobiles. The gatekeeper's solemnity made it seem all the more ridiculous. Corbin decided that the man was suffering from the delusions of advancing age.

In spite of himself, he could not suppress a chuckle. "This is a new one on me," he told the gatekeeper. "I've often been suspected of being a wolf—but never a tiger!" He waved a hand, got the roadster back into motion, and drove toward the house.

A LONG line of large, expensive-looking cars were parked at the upper end of the driveway. Corbin added his roadster to the end of the procession and set out to walk the remaining distance.

The mansion loomed up before him, a huge rambling building of gray sandstone, its many windows glowing with a festive brightness. He began to feel a little nervous. A rising young lawyer, he had grown accustomed to having wealthy people as his clients, but meeting them on a social level was another matter. He decided it was something he had to take in stride—particularly if he intended to see a lot of Doris Melhorn.

It had seemed too good to be true when the invitation had come from Barton Melhorn, Doris' father, to spend the weekend at his home in Sylvan Heights. A short time previously, Corbin had fought to a successful conclusion a stiff legal battle for Melhorn. He had become acquainted with Doris while working on the case, and during the two weeks while the battle had raged in court, their acquaintance had grown into something alive, intimate, and all absorbing. Doris was sweet and unspoiled, with a simplicity and dignity of nature that had appealed to Corbin fully as much as her vivid loveliness.

Corbin had accepted the invitation eagerly. Immediate complications had arisen. Highlight of the weekend was to have a party given by Mrs. Horace Castleton, a wealthy and rather eccentric widow, who though somewhat notorious for her escapades, was renowned for her abilities at entertaining guests. A case had engaged Corbin's attention, which hadn't ended as soon as he expected it would, and it had seemed he wouldn't be able to make the party after all. Melhorn, however—spurred by Doris, as Corbin secretly hoped—had insisted on Corbin's presence, regardless of how late he might arrive. Since Melhorn insisted that the proper arrangements could easily be made, Corbin had given in.

Reaching the steps, Corbin paused a moment to straighten his evening tie and run a hand over his crisp, reddish-brown hair. Then, smoothing down his white flannel jacket, he felt more or less prepared for the ordeal he knew was ahead.

The door was ajar. The servants seemed busy elsewhere. Corbin strode into a huge, brightly lighted hall. Conversation, laughter, and the clinking of glassware drifted to him from a broad doorway ahead and to the right. He walked forward hesitantly, skirting the foot of a massive marble inlaid stairway.

HE FOUND himself looking into a great, lavishly decorated drawing room. The sound of voices washed over him in an almost tangible wave. Unconsciously, he wrinkled his nose against the miasma of liquor and cigarette smoke that filled the room. He ran his eyes over the two score or so of guests scattered about, searching for Doris.

"Oh, there you are! You're Jeffrey Corbin, aren't you?"

Somewhat startled, Corbin found himself looking down at a short, buxom woman in a strapless evening dress of a red color that seemed literally to shriek. Her plump figure was festooned with jewels.

Corbin bowed awkwardly. "And you're Mrs. Castleton?"

"Right the first time." Mrs. Castleton extended a moist, ring-encrusted hand. "Put'er there, Jeff!" The informal formalities over with, Mrs. Castleton put her hands on her broad hips and surveyed Corbin interestedly. "My... Doris must have been holding out on me. She never mentioned that you were so big and good-looking." She laughed loudly at his obvious embarrassment and took his arm. "Come on, Jeff, let me introduce you to the more important of the local gentry."

Except for one in particular, Corbin remembered few if any of the people he met that night. He shook what seemed an endless number of hands, grinned self-consciously into what seemed an endless number of faces, only to carry away the general impression that many of them belonged to persons highly important in political and financial circles. Mrs. Castleton amazed, awed, and bewildered him. Her introductions were accomplished by much backslapping and raucous laughter, interspersed with ribald comments. And between times she kept up a running fire of talk that confused him with its constant change of subjects.

At length, Corbin found himself being led to a corner of the room where a tall, dark man wearing a white turban seemed the focal point of interest for a group of excitedly chattering women.

As they approached the gathering, Mrs. Castleton squeezed Corbin's arm. "And now, Jeff, I want you to meet Dr. Subhas Amkeddar. He's really the most exciting person! Comes from India, you know."

Trailing Corbin in her wake, Mrs. Castleton elbowed her way through the gathering with all the vigor and dexterity of an experienced bargain shopper or football quarterback. Corbin found himself face to face with Dr. Subhas Amkeddar. The polite, somewhat weary smile with which he had prepared himself for the meeting faded from his features. With one of those strange, inexplicable quirks of human nature, he had taken a sudden and violent dislike to the man.

A PSYCHOLOGIST would have been at a loss to explain it clearly. There are instincts involved that are older than the human race, running back to a time when our subhuman ancestors possessed a faculty bordering on a sixth sense, which immediately indicated the presence of an enemy or a friend. Something of that sort may have been involved in Corbin's reaction to Dr. Subhas Amkeddar. He didn't seek to explain it to himself. He didn't even think about it consciously. He only knew, from the instant he set eyes on the Indian, that here was a man to despise, watch, and be wary of.

Dr. Subhas Amkeddar was a spare, elegant figure in faultlessly tailored evening clothes. His features were saturnine, the face long, with gaunt hollows showing under high, jutting cheekbones, the skin leathery and dark with a typical Indian swarthiness. His thin lips were drawn in a politely quizzical smile, but his eyes, deep-set over the hawkish curve of his nose, showed a measuring aloofness in their glittering black depths. They were oddly compelling eyes, holding the glance with a power that was almost hypnotic.

The immediate impression that he gave was one of sleekness, of polished suavity. He seemed a cultured man of the world, well bred, even aristocratic. With his white turban and mahogany skin, he was a veritable personification of the glamorous East. An objectively intent study of his face, however, showed certain other qualities not apparent at once. There was arrogance, a dominating will that sought its ends through craftiness and stealth. There was ruthlessness, a slumbering cruelty that might all too easily be awakened. And there was a suggestion of deep wisdom—but a wisdom of things strange and evil, that were old when the Western world was young.

A change came over Mrs. Castleton as she stood before Amkeddar. Her bearing became subdued, hesitant, almost servile.

The Indian watched her with a trace of condescension, toying with a massive gold ring that he wore on the middle finger of his right hand. The ring, Corbin noticed suddenly, had as its motif the head of a tiger. It seemed an appropriate ornament for Amkeddar to wear; there was something definitely tigerish about him.

Abruptly Corbin remembered the gatekeeper and his fantastic story of roaming tigers. Was there something to it after all? Was there even a connection with Amkeddar? Somehow the idea didn't seem too far-fetched to consider.

As Mrs. Castleton performed the introductions, Amkeddar bowed deeply from the waist, murmuring acknowledgements in a resonant, musical voice that held a noticeable English accent. He didn't seem aware of Corbin's extended hand, managing to give onlookers the impression that his bow was a more than ample recognition of formalities. A faint mockery in his black eyes hinted that he was aware of Corbin's dislike, and that this was his answer to it.

CORBIN dropped his hand awkwardly, realizing that he had been made to look like a fool. His initial, inexplicable dislike for Amkeddar became a savage, overpowering hatred. It was only with an effort that he kept himself from tearing at the other's throat. A warning sense rooted deep in prehistory told him that Amkeddar was dangerous, lethal as a coiled Cobra—something to be destroyed without hesitation or mercy.

There was a strained silence, which neither man made an effort to relieve. Mrs. Castleton filled the chasm between them with a torrent of gushy speech.

"Mr. Corbin came late," she explained confidingly to Amkeddar. "But I'm so glad he could make the party. He's a lawyer, you know. He's spending the weekend—or what's left of it—as a guest of Mr. Melhorn."

Amkeddar's swarthy features showed a sudden interest. "Mr. Barton Melhorn, may I inquire?"

Mrs. Castleton nodded with a quickness that Corbin thought much like that of a servant eager to please. "That's right. You see, Mr. Corbin aided Mr. Melhorn in a frightfully important legal case. Why, I understand that millions of dollars were involved. Isn't that right, Jeffrey?"

Corbin shifted uncomfortably. He was plainly aware that Mrs. Castleton was making a fool of herself. He wondered if Amkeddar had that effect on all women. He much preferred the boisterous, unrestrained Mrs. Castleton of several minutes before to the pathetic, subservient woman of the present. He answered, "Millions of dollars is an exaggeration, I'm afraid. It was actually considerably less than that."

Mrs. Castleton shook his arm in playful chiding. "You're too modest, Jeffrey! How do you expect to win a girl like Doris if you're going to be so shy?"

Amkeddar's interest became more intense. Outwardly he remained casual and urbane, but his black eyes became sharp and predatory.

"Indeed?" he murmured. "Mr. Corbin, I take it, is...ah...romantically inclined toward Miss Melhorn?"

CORBIN'S glance narrowed on the other. He knew suddenly that the question wasn't as innocent as it seemed. The fact that Amkeddar had asked it at all showed he was interested in Doris. He had obviously met her earlier in the evening and had been greatly attracted by her. Corbin became grimly aware that he had a rival in Amkeddar—a rival who was fascinating to women, who gave strong indications of being a person who would stop at nothing to gain his ends.

Corbin wondered in sudden anxiety about Doris. What were her reactions to Amkeddar? Was she as much charmed by him as the others seemed to be?

Beside him, Mrs. Castleton laughed.

"Romantically inclined? From the way Jeffrey's been looking around for Doris ever since he arrived, I'd say that was certainly the case! Well, I'd better not keep him any longer." She excused herself—something she hadn't bothered to do with the other guests—and tugged at Corbin's arm.

The last thing he saw as, he was led away, were Amkeddar's eyes, cold and menacingly hostile. He knew that he had made an enemy.

CHAPTER TWO
Parlor Stunt Sinister

DORIS and her father were chatting with a group of acquaintances at one side of the room when Corbin and Mrs. Castleton finally reached them. Corbin forgot Amkeddar as he saw the welcoming brightness that appeared in Doris' tawny, gold-flecked eyes.

"I'm glad you could get here, Jeff," she said simply. Her soft, slightly husky voice contained a warmth that gave her words a special significance. She was slim and lovely in a simple evening dress of dark green crepe. Her face was fresh and vivid in its frame of lustrous, coppery brown hair.

"I echo Doris' sentiment," Barton Melhorn chuckled, as he shook Corbin's hand. He winked jovially. "That's all I seem to be doing lately, anyway." Melhorn was a little over average height, slender, with a wiry athletic build. He had crisp, grizzled hair, and the keen, dynamic features one would expect of a top-flight business executive.

Mrs. Castleton put in, "Sorry I kept Jeff so long. I wanted him to meet the crowd." She waved a plump hand, once more her old, unrestrained self. "I've got to scoot. It's time I got the entertainment started."

Corbin was not to be left alone with Doris, as he had hoped. Melhorn claimed his attentions for the moment, introducing him to the people with whom he had been conversing. One of them proved to be Melhorn's sister, Nora, a prim-looking spinster, who seemed a feminine edition of Melhorn himself.

Before Corbin completely realized what was happening, he found himself drawn into a discussion of the legal case that he had won for Melhorn. Belatedly remembering Doris, he was dismayed to find that she had moved. His dismay increased when he found her standing a short distance away, about to accept a Martini from a suavely smiling Amkeddar.

Corbin could see Doris' face only in profile. She seemed to be smiling, listening in complete interest to whatever Amkeddar had to say. As Corbin watched, he saw the girl begin to sip from her glass. Amkeddar glanced suddenly in Corbin's direction, his dark face mocking, and his black eyes bright with a strange triumph.

ANGER seared through Corbin. Again he experienced an overwhelming urge to get his hands on Amkeddar's lean throat. With an effort, he got himself under control. Deliberately, he turned his back on Amkeddar and the girl, devoting his attention to the people before him.

Presently, the group broke up. Corbin found himself alone with Melhorn. He asked, "Have you met Dr. Subhas Amkeddar?"

Melhorn smiled wryly. "I'll say I have. The fellow seems to be Mrs. Castleton's particular pet. The same might be said for most of the other women here. Even Nora, my sister, seemed greatly taken with him."

"I gather that you don't think very highly of Dr. Amkeddar," Corbin said, with an answering grin.

"Hardly!" Melhorn grunted. "He's a smooth scoundrel if I ever saw one. I'd say he's well worth keeping a careful eye on."

"What sort of a doctor is he? What's his field?"

"Dashed if I know, Jeff. From what I've heard he's supposed to be a scientist of some kind. Research work. He's been living in Sylvan Heights only a little more than two months. Lives in a large, walled-in estate on Cedar Road, about a half-mile from my place. Just met him tonight, though." Melhorn looked about him slowly, then drew closer to Corbin.

"Don't think me an old gossip, Jeff, but I've talked with several acquaintances about Amkeddar. I've learned some rather interesting things. It seems that he's been receiving a lot of visitors lately. Nothing in that, you might say—but these visits are made late at night, between certain hours, on certain days. Mostly women. The bored, over-moneyed sort who go for anything providing novelty or thrills."

"Do you know what might be going on?"

"No. Something queer, however, you can bet."

A voice rose suddenly above the general hubbub. It was that of Mrs. Castleton, who stood on a chair in the middle of the room.

"Friends, Romans, and gentlemen farmers, lend me your ears! Will everybody please find seats? We're going to have a little fun."

The announcement was followed by an excited murmuring. Mrs. Castleton was widely known for the strange twists in entertainment given at her parties. The guests were curious to know what she had in mind tonight. They sought chairs at the edges of the room in eager haste. A momentary confusion reigned.

CORBIN felt a hand touch his arm as he and Melhorn turned to find seats. It was Doris. He was delighted to have her back at his side, but a restraint held him at the memory of her talking with Amkeddar.

Doris' face was shadowed, strained. Her smile at Corbin seemed to take an effort. "Forgive me for running off, Jeff. I went to say hello to some friends, and Dr. Amkeddar, the lady-killer, collared me. I had to drink a Martini to get rid of him—and I particularly detest Martinis. That one had an awful taste."

Relief swept Corbin. "For a while I thought you were as susceptible to his charms as the other women here. Glad to know I'm wrong."

Doris suppressed a shudder. "Amkeddar leaves me cold, I assure you. There's something nasty and mean about him that… Oh, I can't explain it. But I'm afraid of him, Jeff. The way he looks at me…"

"If he bothers you just let me know," Corbin said grimly. "I'd like an excuse to wipe that smug, superior look off his face."

Most of the people were already seated. Becoming aware of this, Corbin hastily took Doris' arm and led her toward a couple of chairs, which were as yet unoccupied. The babble slowly gave way to an expectant silence.

From her perch on the chair, Mrs. Castleton launched into an explanation of her program. "All right, folks. Tonight we're going to have something a little extra special. The guests themselves are going to provide the fun. I'm going to pass out numbered cards. When a corresponding number is drawn, some lucky guest will have a chance to step out and strut his stuff. Anything goes, as long as it's entertaining and within the limits of Emily Post."

Gasps of delight and cries of dismay followed. Mrs. Castleton's idea was far from being new, but it was novel enough as far as her guests were concerned. They were of the type accustomed to being entertained rather than doing the entertaining themselves.

Servants began to move among the guests, passing out the numbered cards. The drawing room became filled with an atmosphere of nervous anticipation.

"What will you do if your number is called?" Doris asked Corbin.

He frowned deeply in mock-concentration. "Hmmm...I'm a lawyer, so I guess I'll give a burlesque of a courtroom scene, pretending to cross-examine a witness. How about you?"

Doris grimaced. "That's what I'm worrying about. I can play a sizzling game of tennis or golf, fry a mean egg, or read my weight in books, but that's about all. I wish I were able to do something really artistic at times like this. Like playing that beautiful piano Mrs. Castleton has over there. But I've never had enough of an artistic urge to get started. A disappointing person, aren't I?"

"I don't think so," Corbin reassured her. "Artistic women are usually too conceited to be entirely human. I like tennis and golf, and I'm crazy about eggs."

"Not really?" Doris mocked, though her tawny eyes were soft. She spread her hands helplessly. "But what am I going to do, Jeff?"

"Why not pretend to fry an egg? You know—everything wrong."

"That's an idea. I'm in your debt, Jeff."

"I certainly won't forget to collect..."

Mrs. Castleton had climbed down from her chair, and a bowl filled with numbered squares had been placed upon it. She raised her hands for silence.

"All ready now. When your number's called, step into the middle of the room and go into your act. The penalty for failing to produce will be three loud boo's, with everybody joining in."

AMID general laughter and apprehensive comment, she reached into the bowl. The first number called was that of a stout, elderly woman, who gave a quite creditable imitation of a much-publicized moving picture actress. The next, a scholarly-looking, bespectacled young man, obviously stricken with a severe case of self-consciousness, stammered an apology. He was loudly booed. The following victim, a waggish-looking oldster, was more fortunate. He told a joke that was received with much laughter and hand clapping. The tension began to lift as the guests entered more and more into the spirit of the game.

Corbin's enjoyment, however, suffered an early blow. He noticed Amkeddar seated across the room. The Indian was watching Doris. Slyly, pretending an interest in the game, he was drinking in every move she made. His black eyes glittered with a hungry intentness that made Corbin almost squirm with growing anger.

After a moment, Amkeddar became aware of Corbin's scrutiny. Abrupt defiance leaped out on his mahogany-hued features. A latent, yet venomous glare of anger followed. Then as Amkeddar's cunning mind evidently appraised the situation, he smiled ever so slightly in a mocking manner.

It was a challenge, Corbin knew. Amkeddar was admitting his interest in Doris, and was asking in effect what Corbin was going to do about it. Corbin realized he could do nothing in present circumstances without making himself look bad natured, unmannerly, and a fool. Amkeddar knew that. And awareness that the Indian held the upper hand, even though in a purely psychological sense, made Corbin seethe with underlying rage.

The game was in full swing now. One woman sang a popular song. Another danced. Then Mrs. Castleton reached into the bowl again.

"Number twenty-two!" she called out.

Amkeddar rose smoothly to his feet. "That is my number, I believe," With a self-assured smile, he advanced to the middle of the room. A deep silence fell at his appearance. The assemblage watched him with an attentiveness that had not been accorded previous performers. Amkeddar was mystery, romance. In every mind was intense curiosity as to what he would give as his act.

Satisfied that he had the complete interest of his audience, Amkeddar began speaking in confident, resonant tones. "What I shall do will be considered extremely unusual, even questionable. But it will be interesting, and I assure you, quite harmless. I intend to give an exhibition of hypnotism. I shall select as my subject…" He glanced momentarily around the room. "…Miss Doris Melhorn."

Corbin felt a sudden wrench of horror. Doris clutched his arm. "Oh, Jeff!" Her voice was sharp with dismay.

Corbin stood up purposefully. "For personal reasons, I shall have to protest Dr. Amkeddar's choice of Miss Melhorn. Besides, Miss Melhorn herself is averse to the idea. May I suggest that Dr. Amkeddar make another selection?"

MRS. CASTLETON bustled forward. She said chidingly. "Jeffrey, don't be so childish. It's all in fun. Dr. Amkeddar has given his promise that it will be quite harmless. Isn't that right, Doctor?"

Amkeddar nodded with a humoring smile. "Quite right. Mr. Corbin's fears are groundless. I should like to say same for Miss Melhorn."

The guests added their own insistences. Angrily, Corbin realized that Doris had been chosen as a scapegoat. None of the others were willing to be hypnotized. Doris offered each of them a way out.

Against concerted opposition, Corbin was helpless. He gave in. Reseating himself, he glanced at Barton Melhorn, seated in a nearby chair. Melhorn shrugged, frowning. Apparently, he didn't like the idea any more than Corbin did, admitting his own inability to do anything about it.

Like a high priestess leading a victim to sacrifice, Mrs. Castleton took Doris' arm and ushered her to where Amkeddar stood. Then she drew aside.

Amkeddar smiled encouragingly.

"Relax, Miss Melhorn. If your mind is rigid with apprehension, hypnosis will be impossible." In his deep, musical voice, he added further reassurances. The rhythm of his words slowed imperceptibly. Slowly, gradually, his tone took on increasingly depth and power. His black eyes were fixed compellingly upon Doris' tawny ones. It was all very subtle. The girl was being hypnotized even before she completely realized it was taking place.

A cold, heavy lump formed in Corbin's chest. The impossible was happening. Or else scientists were wrong. Or perhaps Amkeddar possessed a forcefulness, an almost superhuman will. Doris didn't want to be hypnotized. Unconsciously, with all her strength, she was resisting. But inexorably Amkeddar was hypnotizing her.

The guests were silent and motionless, fascinatedly watching. Amkeddar's long thin fingers began to writhe and sway like tiny dark snakes before Doris' eyes. He spoke softly, almost inaudibly, murmuring words that Corbin could not understand. Strange, foreign-sounding words. Doris' eyes were wide and unblinking. They seemed a clear, glowing yellow, almost weirdly luminous. Cat's eyes, Corbin thought suddenly. Tiger's eyes. And for an insane moment it seemed to him that the head of a tiger was mirrored in their golden depths. A reflection of Amkeddar—of the will, the spirit, he was imposing on her.

CORBIN got himself in hand. He decided he was imagining things. His anxiety for Doris had made him over-wrought, susceptible to delusions.

Finally Amkeddar dropped his hands and stepped back. Doris stood rigid and unmoving, staring straight before her as though into immense distances.

Amkeddar glanced speculatively about the room. His eyes settled upon the piano. He turned back to Doris.

"Miss Melhorn, can you play the piano?"

Her eyelids did not flicker. "No, I cannot play the piano." Her voice sounded small and remote.

"But you can play if I say that you can."

"Yes, I can play."

"Then you will seat yourself before the piano. You will play—" Amkeddar turned to the watching guests. "Will someone be so kind as to suggest a suitable composition?"

A man named a selection from Chopin. Amkeddar asked Doris, "Are you familiar with this composition, Miss Melhorn?"

"I have heard it, but I cannot recall it clearly."

"You will play it."

"Yes. Doris walked slowly over to the piano and sat down. Her slim fingers poised over the keys. She hesitated a moment, then began to play.

Whispers of astonishment were exchanged among the guests. Doris hadn't been able to play the piano, hadn't remembered clearly the composition that had been named. But she was playing it—and it was beautiful playing.

Corbin's mind flamed with wonder. Something was happening that smacked of magic—something that couldn't be explained in terms of Western knowledge. Science would have said it was impossible. Nothing can come from the human mind that has not already been stored there. But Doris who could not play the piano was playing it; playing a selection from Chopin that was vague in her memory.

Corbin's wonder abruptly vanished as a hand touched his shoulder, startling him. He turned to look into the face of a man seated behind him, leaning forward. The other wore an air of surreptitious confiding. He spoke softly, his voice audible only to Corbin.

"If I were you, I'd watch Dr. Subhas Amkeddar very carefully. A while ago, I saw him drop something into a drink he gave Miss Melhorn."

Corbin was shocked. "You're certain?"

"Positive. I have good eyes, and I'm not a busybody trying to stir up trouble. Dr. Amkeddar is up to something where Miss Melhorn is concerned. Watch him." The man sat back, his features turning impassive.

Corgin felt dazed, stunned. Amkeddar had dropped something into the Martini that Doris had drank. Corbin remembered Doris' remark about the Martini having an awful taste. Did whatever Amkeddar had placed in it explain his complete hypnotic control over Doris? To Corbin, the whole affair suddenly seemed a cunning and shrewdly laid plan. He wondered if Amkeddar hadn't suggested the game to Mrs. Castleton with the idea of exerting his evil influence on Doris.

Fear laid icy fingers upon him. He realized that Amkeddar had just gotten started in whatever devilish scheme he had made. What would he do next?

Doris finished playing the composition. At a command from Amkeddar, she rose. He waved his hands before her face again, murmuring unintelligibly. The alertness of self-will crept back into Doris' eyes. She looked about her bewilderedly, like one having awakened from a deep sleep. Nervously, she nodded at Amkeddar and returned to her chair beside Corbin.

There was a patter of applause. The guests had been entertained more than satisfactorily, and were registering their approval. The sinister nuances of the act had been completely lost upon them.

Corbin asked Doris anxiously, "How do you feel?"

"I can't exactly explain. I feel all right, but my thoughts... It's as though something had stirred them up and they haven't stopped whirling around yet."

Her confused state did not wear off. Made aware of it by Corbin, Melhorn decided that she needed a night's rest. Preparations were made for leaving.

Mrs. Castleton was solicitous. "There's nothing wrong, I hope? It's rather early to leave."

"Doris isn't feeling well," Melhorn explained, a distinct coolness in his voice. "It would really be best for her to be put to bed."

"She's just nervous," Mrs. Castleton said. "She'll be all right in the morning."

Under his breath, Corbin muttered, "She'd better be..."

After a restrained exchange of goodnights, they strode out of the house and toward the line of parked cars. Melhorn rode with his sister, Nora. Corbin followed in his roadster with Doris.

"Feel any better?" Corbin asked after a while, when he felt that the girl had been exposed sufficiently to the cool night air rushing past the speeding car.

"I think so. My mind seems to have calmed a little, anyway. But, Jeff, I think I know what's wrong now. It's as though a part of me had been captured—trapped. And I feel helpless...as if there were things I had to do that I can't remember." She drew closer to him, shivering. "It's all so strange... "Jeff—I'm afraid!"

CHAPTER THREE
Tiger Tracks

A SHRILL cry awakened Corbin. He rose to a sitting position on the bed, instantly awake, listening tensely.

"Barton! Barton!" It was Nora Melhorn's voice, high-pitched with urgent fear.

Corbin heard the patter of feet running down the hall. Then there was the staccato tattoo of knuckles beating against a door.

Barton Melhorn's voice sounded. "Nora? For heaven's sake, what is it?"

"It's Doris! She's...she's gone!"

Corbin listened no further. A hand of ice gripping his heart, he tumbled out of bed and hurried into his robe. As he burst into the hall, he almost collided with the butler and the maid, who had come rushing from their rooms below. Melhorn, framed in the light from his room, was listening to Nora. She was babbling an explanation, her words rushing over each other.

"—worried about her, and I went to her room to see how she was sleeping. And she wasn't there! The windows were open. She must have gone out herself...or...or someone carried her away..."

Noticing Corbin, Melhorn nodded. "You heard?"

"Yes. Where's Doris' room?"

"Downstairs. She preferred it because it opened on the garden."

"Take me there—quick! If we're not too late, we may be able to find some indication of what happened to her."

"Just a moment." Melhorn ducked back into his room. When he reappeared, he was holding a flashlight in one hand and a revolver in the other. He jerked his head at Corbin. "Come on, Jeff."

The door of Doris' room was open. Hurrying in, Melhorn switched on the lights.

Corbin glanced at the bed. It had been slept in, but not otherwise disarranged, as would have happened in case of a struggle. The indications were that Doris had left voluntarily.

Beyond the bed was a line of French windows, partially ajar to permit entrance of the cool night breeze. One of the windows was opened a little more than the others, Corbin noticed. He strode toward it, emerging upon a stone terrace. A large garden spread before him, ghostly in the pale, silver light of the Moon. He turned as he became aware that Melhorn had followed. He asked, "May I borrow your flashlight a moment?"

"Of course, Jeff."

CORBIN climbed over the terrace balustrade and dropped down into the shrubbery below. With the flashlight, he carefully examined the ground. After a moment he released a sharp exclamation of surprise. There were tracks in the soil—footprints of the size that a woman would have made, mingled with the paw prints of an animal. Corbin's lips tightened as he recognized these latter. They were the tracks of a tiger.

Straightening, Corbin related his discovery to Melhorn.

"A tiger!" Melhorn gasped. "You must be mistaken, Jeff. It...it's impossible!"

"Take a look yourself, then."

Melhorn dropped down beside Corbin. He examined the prints with a flashlight, which he had obtained from the butler. His eyes widened. "You're right! Those are tiger tracks. But a tiger—in Sylvan Heights…"

Corbin's lips were stiff and dry. He said quickly, "The gun. Give it to me. We've got to search the garden."

Utter horror dawned in Melhorn's face. "Lord!" he whispered. "Lord! Jeff, you don't think Doris may have been…hurt?"

"I'm afraid to think. I'm going to look—but I'm not going to think. If anything has happened to her…"

Slowly and warily, they began the search, peering into patches of moonlight, probing with their flashlight beams deep shadows among the shrubbery. They saw nothing, heard nothing, indicative of the lurker they sought. There was just the scraping of branches moving in the breeze, the rustling whisper of leaves.

The revolver butt was hard and clammy in Corbin's hand. In his chest was a stifled pounding. Doris, he thought. Doris. If anything had happened to her… He fought down his anxiety in the urgency of the task at hand. He had to be fully alert. Somewhere a tiger might be crouching over its prey. At any moment there might be a deep, animal growl, the swift pad-pad of paws, a lithe, tawny form leaping from the gloom.

But as the tense minutes passed, nothing happened. Corbin and Melhorn returned to their starting point, having made a complete circuit of the grounds surrounding the house. Despite the thoroughness of their search, they had found nothing that would show a struggle had taken place. There were no spatters of blood anywhere, no shreds of torn cloth.

Melhorn said slowly, "I don't know what to make of this, Jeff, unless it's that Doris wandered off somewhere and the tiger followed her."

"But why should she have wandered off in the first place?" Corbin demanded. "It was hardly the time of night for going anywhere. And she wasn't dressed for it. You've seen her footprints. Her feet were bare. For another thing, if the two sets of tracks were made at the same time—as I'm pretty sure they were—instead of at an interval, why should the tiger merely have followed her? Why didn't it attack at once, here, in the garden?"

MELHORN passed a hand over his face in agitated perplexity. "I don't know, Jeff. Lord, I don't know. The whole thing is impossible—insane! A tiger in Sylvan Heights... Doris wandering from her room—"

Corbin's thoughts raced grimly. On the surface, the circumstances of Doris' disappearance were so strange and fantastic as almost to be without meaning. But somewhere, he was sure, were details that would fit everything into a logical pattern. Details that were recent, still fresh in memory, needing only to be sorted out and arranged. Carefully, he went over the events of the previous evening, searching for evidence that would give his vague but inescapable certainty a basis in fact.

Abruptly, almost irrelevantly, he thought of Amkeddar. He stiffened as though from the shock of an electric current, Amkeddar! In a flash of realization, the mystery of Doris' disappearance seemed suddenly clear.

Melhorn gestured helplessly. "There's only one thing left to do, Jeff. We'll have to call in the police. They may be able to find what happened to Doris."

"It won't be necessary to call them," Corbin said. "I'm pretty sure I know where Doris can be found."

"What do you mean?" Melhorn questioned, staring. "How can you possibly know?"

Swiftly, Corbin explained, building up detail by detail a complete picture, which previously his mind had encompassed in an instant. He repeated the strange story about roaming tigers told by the gatekeeper at the Castleton estate, a story borne out by the tracks that he and Melhorn had found in the garden. He mentioned the ring with its tiger head motif worn by Amkeddar, which suggested that the Indian was in some way connected with tigers. And he told of Amkeddar's consuming interest in Doris, which had led him to choose her as a subject for his exhibition of hypnotism, after having previously dropped something into a drink he had given her. He finished:

"Considering these facts, the only place to which Doris could have gone is to where Amkeddar lives. It's all part of a devilish and cunning plan. Doris attracted Amkeddar, but he knew, unlike the other women at the party, that she disliked and feared him. How to remove these feelings? How to make it possible for him to see her? Through hypnotism, of course. But first he had to make her susceptible to his influence, or it wouldn't work. He accomplished this by dropping some sort of drug into her Martini. And once he had her hypnotized—you've heard of post-hypnotic suggestion? Imposing upon a hypnotized person an order which he will follow later, when released from the trance?"

MELHORN nodded jerkily, his face pale and drawn.

"That's why Doris left the house," Corbin went on. "Amkeddar had impressed the command upon her mind while he had her hypnotized. What else would explain it? Why else would she have gone out at this time of the night, in her bare feet?"

"But the tiger tracks, Jeff. How do you explain them?"

Corbin said with grim earnestness, "The tiger was sent to see that Doris did what she was supposed to do, or to lead her to where she was supposed to go."

"Why, that's utterly impossible!" Melhorn protested unbelievingly. "Jeff, have you gone mad?"

"Not at all. Look here, I'm not an expert tracker, but I'm quite certain that the prints we found of Doris and the tiger were made at the same time. All right, if it was an ordinary kind of tiger, why wasn't Doris attacked? The fact that she wasn't, the fact that a tiger should be present in Sylvan Heights at all, shows it wasn't an ordinary kind of tiger. Is it too fantastic, then, to suppose that its purpose had been to lead her somewhere?"

Melhorn ran a hand agitatedly through his hair. "Lord, I don't know! But, Jeff, you think that Amkeddar is mixed up in it?"

"I'm positive."

"Then we'd better call the police…"

Corbin laughed shortly. "Do you think they'd believe our reasons for wanting them to search Amkeddar's home? They'd think we were either drunk or crazy. At best, they only send someone here to check our story. That would waste too much time. No—if anything is going to be done about Amkeddar, we'll have to do it ourselves."

"But what can we possibly do, Jeff?"

"We'll drive over to Amkeddar's place and tell him that Doris has disappeared—apparently having wandered away in her sleep. We'll explain that we came to him because we thought his hypnotizing of Doris may have been responsible. That'll give us an excuse to search his house. If nothing else, our suspicions will warn him to leave Doris alone."

Melhorn straightened purposefully. "All right. I'll get dressed."

"Meet me in ten minutes," Corbin said. "We'll take my car."

CHAPTER FOUR
Dr. Amkeddar Is Unwilling

MELHORN pointed through the windshield of the speeding roadster. "There, Jeff. That's where Amkeddar lives."

Corbin nodded, squinting through the glare of the headlights. Down the road ahead, drawing swiftly closer, loomed a high concrete wall. It looked grim and forbidding, the sort of wall that might very well have encircled a prison. Hardly as neat and well tended, however, it was striated with cracks and covered thickly with vines.

Corbin smiled thinly. "That wall is just what I'd have expected of Amkeddar. Anything could go on behind it, and nobody would be the wiser."

Reaching the wall, he slowed the roadster. Presently he saw an opening about halfway down its length, barred by a high iron gate. Beside the gate, he drew to a stop. He eyed the barrier calculatingly a moment, then glanced at Melhorn.

"I'd like to get in without giving Amkeddar a chance to cover up. The gateman is certain to obtain his approval before admitting us."

Melhorn said quietly, "This should help, Jeff." He extended the revolver.

Corbin took it, the lines of his face tight and determined. Dropping the gun into a pocket of his jacket, he slipped from the car and strode up to the gate. A large house bulked like a sleeping monster on the grounds beyond. No lights showed behind its many windows. Nearby was a smaller building, which to Corbin seemed too large to be a garage. Light glowed behind a small, barred window set high in one wall.

In the illumination of the moon, the grounds looked wild and unkept, almost jungle-like. Corbin wondered if Amkeddar was as neglectful about other aspects of his living conditions. Or was there a purpose in his leaving the grounds untended? Something connected with his experiments?

Corbin returned his thoughts to the problem of getting through the gate. Climbing over was out of the question, as Melhorn wouldn't have been able to make it. And if Amkeddar had guards posted—a not too remote possibility—Corbin didn't want to take the risk of getting shot. Being admitted seemed the best way. But how to attract the attention of the gatekeeper without warning Amkeddar of his presence?

His problem was unexpectedly solved. Materializing like a wraith out of the darkness, a man moved abruptly into sight behind the gate, startled him.

THE headlights of the roadster, pointing down the road, provided enough illumination for Corbin to make out details. The man he saw was an Indian like Amkeddar, hawk-featured and swarthy, a turban wound about his head. Corbin realized that the man must have been patrolling the grounds, having been attracted by the lights of the car. Corbin wondered grimly why Amkeddar should have guards on duty. What was he trying to protect—or hide?

His awareness centered sharply on the guard. The other inclined his turbaned head slightly, liquid dark eyes calculating and alert.

"What *Sahib* want?" he asked in a soft, accented voice.

Corbin said, "I'd like to see Dr. Amkeddar. It's very important."

"If *Sahib* will give name..."

"That and the nature of my business is something I can tell only Dr. Amkeddar."

"Much regret, *Sahib*. *I* have order. You must give name."

Corbin decided that his pretended mysteriousness needed a little acting to make it more effective. He glanced fearfully up and down the road, then turned back to the guard as though unable to conceal any longer his impatience and anxiety. "Listen—we're wasting precious time. This is a matter of life or death, I tell you. I must see Dr. Amkeddar at once. Later you may be sorry that you kept me waiting so long."

The Indian fondled his lower lip indecisively. Finally he shook his head. "I have order, *Sahib*. I must tell Master, give name."

Corbin glanced at the road again. His assumed impatience turned suddenly to a display of anger. "Are you stupid?" he demanded. "It would take too long to tell Dr. Amkeddar. I can't wait out here on the road, in plain sight. At least you could let me in—where I'll be safe."

The guard shuffled his feet in a turmoil of doubt. Sensing an advantage, Corbin reached quickly for his billfold, removed a large bill, and thrust it through the gate.

"Look—I'll take the blame, but if Dr. Amkeddar should still be angry with you, this should make it easier. I've just got to see Dr. Amkeddar at once."

The Indian eyed the bill with evident greed. As though drawn to it irresistibly, his lean dark hand reached out. Then he suddenly snatched it back. The greed vanished from his face, leaving stark fear. "No...I cannot. I cannot! The Master, he would...he—" The Indian broke off, his face working like one who has seen a vision of nightmare horror.

A FINGER of ice seemed to draw itself along Corbin's spine. Thoughtfully, he replaced the bill. In the guard's reaction he saw a hand that was harsh and cruel, utterly without mercy and tolerance. The influence of Amkeddar over his servants revealed new insight on the character of the man.

Plainly, admission was not to be accomplished by guile. That left only one thing to do, if Amkeddar were still to be taken by surprise. In a swift movement, Corbin pulled the revolver from his pocket and leveled it at the guard.

"I told you I haven't any time to waste. This will prove it. Now—are you going to let me in, or do I have to shoot holes in your legs to force you?"

The Indian looked at the gun. His features cleared in something that was almost relief. He had been given a way out. His orders did not hold up under an immediate threat of being crippled. Producing a key from a pocket of his rough, dark suit, he unlocked the gate.

Gesturing the guard into the car beside Melhorn, Corbin mounted the running board, revolver pointed alertly. Melhorn drove up a long gravel driveway, drawing to a stop before the larger of the two buildings. Corbin prodded the Indian out before him and strode to the door. After a moment's search he found the bell and pressed it. Tensely he waited. The guard stood by, stolidly quiet.

A muffled growl lifted suddenly on the night air. Despite his preparedness for anything in the way of danger, Corbin's muscles perked. That had been an animal growl, he realized—the sort of sound that a tiger would have made. As he listened, the growl was repeated. It came, he discovered, from the adjoining, small building. He recalled the lighted window he had seen while at the gate.

An abrupt clicking noise from behind the door brought Corbin whirling around. The portal swung open. Light from the hall showed a woman standing at the threshold. Like Amkeddar and the guard, she was an Indian. A scarlet *sari* had been thrown hastily over her shoulders and draped over her long, glistening black hair. She was attractive in a mature, darkly exotic way.

The woman looked inquiringly from the guard to Corbin. Then she saw the gun in Corbin's hand. Her large, liquid eyes widened slightly, but whatever she felt of surprise and fear was well controlled.

"What is the meaning of this?" she asked quietly. Her English was faultless. It contained nothing of the studied British accents affected by Amkeddar.

In some inexplicable way, Corbin found himself drawn to the woman. Her eyes were steady and clear, her bearing eloquent of a character too frank and courageous to have in it anything of evil. He said, "I want you to take me to Dr. Amkeddar. It's very important."

"May I ask why you should need a gun?"

CORBIN grinned slightly. "My reason for wanting to see him is that important. I can't waste any time on formalities. Everyone insists on making me wait."

The woman said, "Dr. Amkeddar is in the...his laboratory. He is at work."

"The building over there?"

She nodded slowly.

Corbin gestured with the gun. It was his intention to march the woman and the guard to the laboratory building. The next instant he stiffened, his plan forgotten. From the direction of the laboratory had come the sound of a closing door. Then followed the crunch of feet on gravel. Amkeddar moved into view, hurrying toward the house. At sight of Corbin and Melhorn, in the doorway, he stopped.

"Who...why, it's Mr. Corbin! And Mr. Melhorn! I thought I heard a car drive up. This is a nice surprise." As he approached, he became suddenly aware of the gun in Corbin's hand. He gave no indication of being alarmed or otherwise disconcerted. Apparently he had already realized that the presence of Corbin and Melhorn at the house, without his being warned of their arrival meant that they had used force to gain entry.

"Do you usually arm yourself with a gun when calling on people, Mr. Corbin?" he said with thinly veiled sarcasm.

"That depends on the people," Corbin said.

Amkeddar's thin lips lifted in a sardonic smile. In the light streaming through the open doorway he looked like a grimly amused Satan. "That, I take it, is a sample of what is termed repartee. Very witty…I am not unacquainted with American laws, Mr. Corbin. Since you are a lawyer, I need hardly point out that this invasion of my property is anything but legal."

Corbin jerked his shoulders impatiently. "I'm fully aware of the matter. Your property is safe enough. What I'm here for is something that doesn't belong to you—which gives me sufficient justification for my actions."

"Indeed? And what might that be?"

"Doris. Where is she? What have you done with her?"

Amkeddar arched his black brows. "Doris? I presume you mean Miss Doris Melhorn?"

"I don't mean anyone else," Corbin grunted.

"I fear that I do not understand. Are you insinuating that I have done something with Miss Melhorn?"

"I'm more than fairly certain that you have. Doris vanished from her room earlier in the night. Indications are that she did so under some abnormal mental condition. Only one thing could have been responsible for that—the hypnotic trance into which you placed her at Mrs. Castleton's party. I happen to know that posthypnotic suggestion—"

AMKEDDAR had suddenly raised his hand. His cool suavity was gone. "A moment, Mr. Corbin. You speak of matters which might all too easily be misunderstood by servants."

"Servants?" a soft voice inquired, inquired with an ironic inflection. It was the woman who had spoken. Her dark eyes were fixed intently upon Amkeddar. "Can it be, my lord and master, that there are things that you seek to hide from me?"

Amkeddar said harshly, "That will do, Kumara! Return to your room at once." He turned to the guard.

"Chondhas, back to your post!"

"Hold it!" Corbin snapped. "I'll give the orders, if you don't mind. I want these people where I can watch them."

"Do not be melodramatic, Mr. Corbin. I give you my promise that they will not interfere with you in any way."

"Your promise means nothing to me. I'll be certain they're harmless only as long as I can see them."

Abrupt fury twisted Amkeddar's saturnine features into a demoniac mask. He took a step forward, lips writhing back from his teeth, lean dark hands outspread like talons.

Expecting an attack, Corbin settled into a crouch. He watched Amkeddar bleakly, his face craggy with bunched muscles. He held the gun as though no longer aware of it, as though dominated by some primeval battle instinct of fang and claw.

There was an interval of tense, strained silence.

Slowly, Amkeddar relaxed. He began toying with the massive tiger-head ring, which he wore on the middle finger of his right hand. His black eyes smoldered malevolently. Desperation, a trapped impotent rage, showed in the set of his face.

Corbin said slowly, "You are trying to hide something. And it involves Doris. I'm convinced that you know what happened to her tonight—that you know where she is right now."

Amkeddar shook his turbaned head doggedly. "You jump to conclusions, Mr. Corbin. If I gave the impression of trying to hide something, the explanation is simply that I did not wish Kumara to know that I had…ah…broken a certain promise. This was never to practice hypnotism outside of my researches. Is that not right, Kumara?"

The woman moved her shoulders.

"In that one respect, yes."

"I merely wished to provide entertainment at Mrs. Castleton's party," Amkeddar went on, his voice quickening with renewed confidence. "When my number was called during the course of the game, the idea of giving an exhibition of hypnotism was the first to come to my mind. I had no time to think of anything else."

"Then why did you make Doris susceptible to hypnotism by placing a drug in the Martini you gave her before the game began?" Corbin demanded flatly.

A FLICKER that might have been dismay crossed Amkeddar's face, but is was hidden almost instantly behind an expression of injured indignation. "That is a lie," he snapped. "A filthy lie!"

"And why were there the tracks of a tiger below the terrace near Doris' room?" Corbin pursued relentlessly. "Tracks, incidentally, which seem to have been made at the same time as Doris'? What sort of a tiger was it merely to have followed her, instead of attacking right then and there? Was it a special, trained pet of yours, Dr. Amkeddar—sent to make sure she carried out the post-hypnotic suggestion which you planted in her mind at Mrs. Castleton's party?"

Amkeddar said nothing. His face was impassive, a saturnine visage that might have been carved from some fine-grained, hard dark wood. Beneath lowered lids his eyes held a deadly, intent glitter.

The woman, Kumara, stared unseeingly into the darkness beyond the flood of light that poured through the open doorway. Her full lips had a bitter, sullen droop.

Corbin said softly, "Doris is in your laboratory, isn't she, Dr. Amkeddar?"

The Indian stiffened. "This farce has continued long enough, Mr. Corbin. I demand that you leave at once—or I warn you that I shall prosecute to the fullest extent of the law."

Corbin raised the gun, jerking it in a gesture. "The key to your laboratory, Dr. Amkeddar. Give it to me."

"I refuse. I am in the midst of certain experiments that would be ruined by an intrusion at this point. My work involves the glands of living animals. Startling them or angering them would spoil many weeks of labor."

"The key! Are you going to give it to me—or do I have to put a bullet into each of your legs to force you?"

"You...you would hardly dare!"

"Wouldn't I?" Corbin pointed the revolver at Amkeddar's right thigh. His finger began to tighten on the trigger.

There was an abrupt rustle of motion. The guard, Chondhas, had seized the opportunity to leap forward. His arm flashed down in a chopping stroke, the edge of his hand sharply striking the back of Corbin's wrist.

It was a shrewd blow, cleverly placed. Corbin's arm went numb up to the elbow. The revolver dropped from his involuntarily splayed fingers.

Amkeddar pounced upon the weapon with frantic haste. Clutching it warningly in his hand, he straightened, thin lips stretched wide in a grin of malicious triumph. "From now on, *I* give the orders, Mr. Corbin!"

CHAPTER FIVE
Lady—or Tiger?

DISMAY was a sick ache inside Corbin. With bitter self-reproach, he realized that he should never have taken his eyes off Chondhas. By having underestimated the man, he had lost every advantage.

If their positions hadn't so unexpectedly been reversed, he could have forced Amkeddar to show him the laboratory. And if Doris were held captive inside—as he was poignantly certain—Amkeddar could have been charged with kidnapping, his sinister influence permanently removed.

But now—the opportunity was gone. Nor would a new one present itself. Amkeddar had had a narrow escape from detection. And he had been fully appraised as to what Corbin suspected or knew. Thus if he were determined to continue his evil machinations, he was certain to be so painstakingly careful that the difficulties of proving anything against him would be enormous.

Concern for Doris filled Corbin with a cold desolation. What would now become of the girl? Would...would he ever see her again? Raging despair surged through him at the thought. His eyes sharpened on Amkeddar as he experienced a wild desire to leap at the man in frenzied defiance of the revolver he held.

The triumph had faded from the Indian's hawkish, dark face. He was glancing from Corbin to Melhorn, black brows drawn in a speculative frown. The gun followed the movements of his eyes like a swaying snake, prepared at any instant to strike.

40

Kumara moved to Amkeddar's side. She demanded, "What are you going to do?"

"Nothing so obvious as outright murder, of course. You can set your mind to rest on that point." Amkeddar's frown deepened momentarily. Then his thin lips rose at one corner in a hard smile. "There has been much unpleasantness. If our two visitors were to forget what has occurred..."

"You mean to hypnotize—?"

"Watch your tongue!" Amkeddar snapped.

Kumara's liquid dark eyes showed a flash of repressed anger. She hesitated a moment, then began to speak in a soft, musical foreign language. Amkeddar, speaking in the same dialect, heatedly disagreed with whatever she had outlined. An argument followed. Corbin couldn't understand what was being said. But it seemed clear to him that Amkeddar was insisting upon some course of action to which Kumara was opposed.

CORBIN speculated on the relationship between the pair. Whatever is was, Kumara seemed quite free to voice her own mind. And right now she was doing so with great vigor and courage. She gave every indication of possessing a forcefulness of character equal to Amkeddar's. But her's seemed one of honesty and forthrightness, while Amkeddar's suggested trickery and stealth. On the surface it appeared a highly incompatible combination. Corbin wondered about the underlying facts that provided a common basis.

The unintelligible controversy suddenly ended. Amkeddar fell silent, watching Corbin and Melhorn in a sort of baleful contemplation. Finally he nodded, obviously having reached some decision. His glittering black eyes sharpened purposefully. He said, "I shall be lenient. You have forcibly invaded my premises and threatened me with bodily harm. Yet I shall overlook this, understanding the fears for Miss

Melhorn's safety that motivate you. In coming to me with your fears and suspicions, however, you have embarked on a fool's quest. I know nothing of Miss Melhorn's whereabouts. And now I shall have to ask you to leave. You have entered by force. If necessary, I shall have every right to eject you by force."

Melhorn said, "You're forgetting or deliberately overlooking something, Dr. Amkeddar."

"And what is that, if I may ask, Mr. Melhorn?"

"The police. If you're so completely guiltless, you can have us arrested, you know."

"I see no reason to bring the police into this. No harm has been done. The...ah...the score, as I see it, is even."

"So, if you're hiding something," Corbin said, "you wouldn't want to take the chance that an investigation by the police would lose you the game."

Amkeddar's black eyes flashed wrathfully. "You're a fool, Mr. Corbin. Your mind is a hodge-podge or legal technicalities and childish fancies. Enough, I say!" He jerked the revolver in a peremptory gesture at the roadster.

"Get in."

CORBIN hesitated, lips tightening. But the revolver was unwaveringly pointed. A leap could only mean certain death. The tense set of his shoulders left him. With a dejected glance at Melhorn, he walked to the car and slowly climbed in. When Melhorn had followed, Amkeddar and Chondhas mounted the running board on either side, and Corbin sent the roadster moving down the driveway toward the gate.

At the end of the driveway, Amkeddar swung off, standing guard while Chondhas opened the gate. He bowed mockingly, gesturing toward the road. "This way out. Good night..."

With a growl of fury, Corbin sent the roadster careening down the road in a defiant burst of speed. He drove with reckless violence; lips compressed whitely, eyes blazing with rage. Melhorn slumped in his seat, apathetically unresponsive.

Reaching the main highway, Corbin slowed to a stop. He fumbled through his jacket for his cigarettes, tapped one out, then belatedly remembering his manners, passed the pack to Melhorn. They lighted up, smoked in brooding silence.

Finally Corbin muttered, "If only I hadn't been so careless..."

"You did your best, Jeff," Melhorn comforted dully.

"But Doris—"

"We could go to the police. It might not be too late."

"They wouldn't find anything. Amkeddar would be expecting a move like that."

"Then what else—"

Corbin tossed his cigarette away, straightening sharply. "Just thought of something. We're going back. As far as the gate anyway."

Melhorn stared. "What", what do you intend to do?"

"See if an idea of mine is any good. It may not pan out, but it won't do any harm to take a chance." He switched off the car lights, waiting a moment until his eyes became adjusted to the illumination of the setting moon. It was almost dawn. No cars had passed on the highway, and there were certain to be none on Cedar Road. Driving without lights would be almost completely without danger. The road would show up clearly enough in such moonlight as was left.

He turned the roadster around, sent gliding almost silently in the direction from which they had come. His pulses quickened. If he were right, the odds would shift in his favor. Amkeddar would logically expect him to turn to the police. Thus if Doris were held prisoner in the laboratory, Amkeddar would have to hide her somewhere safely beyond the walls of his estate.

He was going to watch the gate. If a car came through, it wouldn't be too difficult to follow...

THE roadster crept stealthily along the dim concrete ribbon. Presently the familiar wall rose grayly in the gloom ahead. Corbin spotted a dense thicket bordering the road and sent the roadster lurching and bumping through a convenient though narrow opening. He left the car, moving to a spot several feet away from where he could see anyone leaving the gate.

Melhorn joined him. They squatted together in the sheltering foliage, waiting.

Minutes like eternities dragged by. The moon was dropping toward the horizon. With its going would come the intense darkness that precedes dawn. Corbin began watching the moon, worrying greatly. If it got too dark, following another car without lights would be dangerous.

Within seconds, his silent pleas were answered. A metallic clicking sounded, followed by a protesting squeal. The gate was being opened!

Just enough light was left. Just enough. Corbin craned forward with a fierce eagerness, narrowed eyes filtering the gloom.

There was no hum of a motor, no whirring of wheels on gravel. Instead, Corbin stifled a gasp of astonishment.

A tiger padded lithely through the gate. It paused in the middle of the road, swiveling its sleek head about as if in uncertainty. It whined softly, a queerly anxious sound. Then it turned toward the undergrowth on the side of the road opposite Corbin's, glided through it, and was gone.

The gate hinges squealed again. There was the clicking of the lock being secured. Then—silence.

Corbin glanced at Melhorn, frowning.

Melhorn whispered, "A tiger, Jeff! What on earth is Amkeddar doing—letting pussy out for the night? Or is there something important behind it?"

"It wasn't what I expected, at any rate," Corbin muttered.

"What did you hope to see?" Corbin asked tersely.

"Perhaps they left before we got back," Melhorn said. "They might have gone in the opposite direction on Cedar Road."

Corbin shook his head. "I don't think so. Amkeddar would have had to be mighty fast. There wasn't much time between our departure and return. No—I'm certain they haven't left yet." Corbin stood up, glancing around. "We'll wait a while longer—and we'd better do it in the car. It isn't safe out here with a tiger roaming about. If anyone leaves, we'll hear it."

In the car, Corbin leaned on the steering wheel, listening. His fingers idly stroked the horn release. A mere outlet for his nerves, yet it gave him an idea. If the tiger were to find them, he thought, a blast from the horn would scare it away. But then—no, it wasn't such a good idea after all. Amkeddar would be warned of their presence.

He scowled in mounting anxiety. Doris... Why didn't Amkeddar show up? If only the tiger wouldn't come nosing around...

THE tiger—and the tiger tracks below the terrace, near the windows of Doris' room. Was it the same tiger, he wondered? Why had it so mysteriously been let out? Had it been sent somewhere?

A few things seemed certain. The gateman at the Castleton estate had known what he was talking about. Tigers *did* roam Sylvan Heights at night. And Amkeddar was definitely responsible for it. But—what was the man up to? What was the reason behind the whole incredible business?

The moon was gone. The intense pre-dawn darkness closed in around the car. On the horizon to the east, the sky began to gray.

Melhorn stretched stiffly. "Doesn't look like Amkeddar's going anywhere, Jeff."

"We could have returned with the police long ago," Corbin agreed. His voice was leaden with disappointment. "If Amkeddar took any precautions against that, they weren't what I thought they'd be."

Melhorn said slowly, "Perhaps Amkeddar didn't have Doris in his laboratory after all, Jeff. Perhaps it was something else he was trying to hide."

"But he knows what happened to Doris. Everything points to him."

"It seems so. Anyway, Jeff, there's nothing to be gained by waiting any longer. Amkeddar has had more than enough time to prepare his defenses."

Corbin sighed and nodded. "We'll return to the house, then. A search of the grounds by daylight may turn up something to give us a fresh start." He switched on the lights of the car, sent it bumping and swaying back onto the road.

Dawn was breaking when Corbin pulled to a stop before the Melhorn residence. He climbed stiffly from the car, and in dismal silence followed Melhorn up the steps to the door.

As Melhorn fumbled abstractedly for his keys, the door suddenly opened. The smooth, round face of the butler grinned out at them. He said, "I was waiting for you to return, sir. I have good news."

Melhorn stared in surprise. "Good news?"

"Yes, sir. Miss Doris has returned safely."

Corbin jerked into startled rigidity.

Melhorn gasped, "Doris—returned? When? How long ago?"

"About an hour, sir. Miss Nora and Dr. Lorrimer are with her now."

Corbin's thoughts raced furiously. Had he been wrong? Was it possible that Doris had been nowhere near Amkeddar's estate? He and Melhorn had been watching Amkeddar's gate for more than an hour. Nothing except a tiger had gone through.

Only a tiger. An animal. Nothing human. But Doris *had* been locked in Amkeddar's laboratory. Of this he was piercingly, unshakably certain. For Doris to have returned could only mean...

HIS mind flamed abruptly with a volcanic realization. Something hinted at by Mrs. Castleton's gateman returned to him with stunning force. Something about people who might be tigers... Which might be taken to mean people who could change—or he changed—into tigers.

Nonsense! Sheer insanity! And yet...

A tiger had gone through Amkeddar's gate. And Doris had returned.

CHAPTER SIX
A Change of Heart

A SMALL shaded lamp on a dressing table lighted Doris' room dimly. Nora Melhorn stood near the French windows, talking in whispers to a short stocky man whom Corbin decided was Dr. Lorrimer. He ignored the pair for the moment as he left Melhorn's side and crossed swiftly over to the bed.

Doris was asleep. Her features seemed a trifle drawn and pale, but otherwise her appearance was reassuring enough.

She looked somehow like a tired little girl, huddled under the covers, her coppery-brown hair tumbled in disarray over the pillow.

Relief swept Corbin. Looking at the girl, knowing she was safe, made the grim events of the past few hours seem suddenly trivial.

Then he noticed that her hands had been lightly bandaged. Nothing serious, apparently. Scratches, at the most. But bandages…

A memory leaped into his mind like a picture thrown on a screen. The memory of a tiger padding lithely across the road and disappearing into the undergrowth that bordered it. Something heavy and cold turned over inside him. Rocks and sharp twigs would have been strewn thickly in the tiger's path through the fields. And Doris wore bandages…

He became aware of Melhorn standing beside him. Their glances met. Relief showed on the older man's face, but his eyes were dark with the shadow of a dreadful suspicion. Quite evidently, he too had noticed the bandages. If he had not already arrived at the same conclusion as Corbin, he seemed well on the way to doing so.

Nora Melhorn glided up, motioning for quiet.

Melhorn whispered, "How did Doris get back?"

"I don't know, Barton. I looked in several times, and then I found her lying there. She was a sight! Hands and feet all wet and covered with mud. I tried to question her, but she seemed unable to remember anything." Nora gestured toward the door. "Now you'd better leave. I'll watch Doris."

Melhorn nodded and beckoned to Corbin and Lorrimer. He led them to the library, where he introduced Lorrimer to Corbin and set about making drinks.

When they had been settled in chairs, Melhorn asked Lorrimer, "Well, George, how is she?"

"Nothing seriously wrong, as far as I could discover," Lorrimer responded. He was pleasant-featured in a blunt, heavy way. His main distinction seemed to be a hirsute one, for his hair, mustache, and eyebrows were all thick, bristling, and almost startlingly black.

"But the bandages—?" Melhorn pursued.

"Just minor scratches. On the palms of her hands and the soles of her feet." Lorrimer studied his glass a moment. The action, to Corbin, seemed oddly evasive. Lorrimer obviously knew something that he didn't intend to reveal just then—if at all. Finally Lorrimer looked up, meeting Melhorn's gaze. "What's it all about anyway, Barton? Nora wasn't very coherent, I'm afraid."

MELHORN glanced hesitantly at Corbin.

Corbin said, "With your permission—?" At Melhorn's nod, he launched into a swift, concise account of the events surrounding Doris' temporary disappearance. He began with the circumstances of the disappearance itself, mentioning his and Melhorn's suspicions of Amkeddar, based on the hypnotizing of Doris by the Indian at Mrs. Castleton's party and the drug which previously he had dropped into Doris' Martini. Then Corbin detailed the expedition to Amkeddar's estate and its outcome. He said nothing of the incredible conclusion to which he had come, linking Doris' return to the tiger that he and Melhorn had seen leaving Amkeddar's gate. He felt impelled to trust Lorrimer, but thought it wisest to state only facts. The implications were there—if Lorrimer were shrewd enough to detect them. To have stated them boldly would only have emphasized their utter bizarreness, to the extent of casting serious doubts on Corbin's motives.

Lorrimer toyed musingly for a moment with his empty glass. Finally he glanced at Corbin from under the cliff-like overhang of his thick black brows and said slowly, "Your story contains hints of something…well, disturbing. I don't intend to discuss it. You carefully avoided doing so yourself, I noticed. It's that sort of a subject, apparently. But I do want to comment on one detail of what you have told me—the numerous references to tigers."

Corbin said eagerly, "You know something?"

"Not exactly. Only to the extent that I've heard rumors about night-roaming tigers myself. A doctor's work takes him among all classes of people, you know. And people like to talk. The strange thing is, however, that the only ones who to my knowledge have mentioned seeing or hearing about tigers are those of the serving class—domestic help, farmers, and such." Lorrimer nodded at Corbin. "Mrs. Castleton's gateman, yes. Obviously, the majority of the wealthy residents of Sylvan Heights have not seen or heard about the tigers, or if they have are strangely inclined not to discuss them."

Lorrimer set his glass on a nearby table and leaned forward in increased earnestness. "Now why should this be? It is evident that the rumors are too striking, too prevalent, to escape notice. Is it that these wealthy residents know something about the tigers that they are trying to hide? If so, what is it? I wouldn't care to hazard a guess, but one thing seems certain—Dr. Subhas Amkeddar is involved.

"At least two things point to him. The first is that he is somehow connected with the tiger rumor. This is borne out by your own discovery—the tiger you saw leaving his estate."

"Also by a ring with a tiger-head insignia, which Amkeddar wears on the middle finger of his right hand," Corbin put in.

Melhorn said, "If I may be permitted to add still another reason. It's that Amkeddar seems to play host to a large group of visitors at odd hours of the night. Usually quite late—and on certain days. These visitors are…well, of the wealthy class. Mostly women. The sort who are always searching for thrills."

LORRIMER nodded his bushy black head. "The fourth thing, then. Lately I've had occasion to examine a number of wealthy class patients…routine check-ups, minor illnesses, and the sort. On the left arms of more than a few I found small red marks in various stages of healing. Marks that could only have been left by the insertion into a vein of a hypodermic needle. Drugs?" Lorrimer jerked one shoulder in a gesture of bafflement. "I could find none of the symptoms of ordinary narcotics. Anyway, Doris has such a mark on her left arm."

Corbin shot forward in his chair. "Doris? You're certain?"

"Quite. And it was made very recently—hardly more than three or four hours ago. From what you've told me of Dr. Subhas Amkeddar dropping something into Doris' drink, and the rest, it seems that he's the most likely candidate among persons who might be responsible. And that, of course, would mean that he was responsible also for the marks on the arms of the other persons I mentioned."

Melhorn rose angrily to his feet. "Then what in the name of reason are we waiting for? We have enough on the man right now to put him safely beyond creating further harm."

Lorrimer shook his head slowly, almost sadly. "We know this much—but what could we charge him with? Illegal use of drugs? What sort of drugs? They left no symptoms that I could recognize and it's certain that no other medical man could either. Unless we can be definite about this, we might as well not waste our time. The police don't act on mere suspicion, you know.

"Kidnapping?" Lorrimer went on. "But Doris has returned. And as far as I could make out, she hasn't been harmed. Are there any facts that could be used in court to show that Dr. Subhas Amkeddar actually was behind her temporary disappearance?

"Threatening public safety by being responsible for the roaming tigers? But has anyone been hurt? Despite the fact that many persons have glimpsed tigers, the police would laugh at the story unless concrete proof of the tigers and their danger could be produced."

Lorrimer shook his head again. "And there's another and quite important point to consider. Dr. Subhas Amkeddar seems intimately connected with a sizeable group of influential people. Probably they are backing him in whatever he is up to. I don't know. But if they were to put pressure on the authorities, no charge we pinned on him would stick unless it was conclusive beyond any slightest doubt."

"I agree with that," Corbin said grimly. "But it can't be entirely hopeless. There must be something we can go on. Amkeddar's work, for example. He's supposed to be doing research on animal glands—and the state recently passed an anti-vivisection law. If we knew for certain—"

LORRIMER'S stocky form had grown rigid with sudden excitement. "I think you've hit on something. As I said a while ago, a doctor gets around, hears things. Well, numerous persons have told me that Dr. Subhas Amkeddar has been buying a large quantity of livestock—cattle, sheep, and goats. And on at least two occasions, persons driving past his place late at night have heard the screams of animals, and also…growls."

"Tiger growls?" Corbin asked quickly.

"They weren't specific. Just growls. But since Dr. Amkeddar seems more or less definitely linked to tigers, I'd say that was possible." Lorrimer's heavy black brows drew together in a frown. "I don't see that this helps much, however. If Amkeddar is in some way breaking the anti-vivisection law, nothing much could be done to him—a monetary fine at the most."

"But," Corbin pointed out, "if all we wanted was an excuse to get the police to search his estate, that would be plenty. The police might ignore the tiger or drug angles because they can't be backed up by proof. But this is something definite. It's generally known that Amkeddar is doing some kind of research work on animal glands. Records could be shown that Amkeddar has been buying animals— quite obviously for his experiments. And witnesses could be produced to testify to hearing animal screams, issuing from his estate. The police couldn't ignore these facts. They'd have to agree on a search."

Lorrimer's frown deepened. "I can't see what good a mere search would accomplish."

"Amkeddar's research work may be just a blind," Corbin explained incisively. "Actually he may be up to something entirely different. Something…well…devilish. And if the police were unexpectedly to walk in on him, looking for one thing, but only to find another—"

"That's it," Melhorn exclaimed, bringing his palm down with a sharp sound on the arm of his chair. "While we were at his place, Jeff, I had the distinct impression that he was hiding something in that laboratory of his. Not Doris—if she had actually been inside—but something else."

Lorrimer glanced curiously at Corbin. "You seem to have something there. What do you intend to do?"

"That depends on Amkeddar. I'm not one to interfere with matters that are no business of mine, but if he doesn't leave Doris alone, I'll do everything in my power to put him behind bars."

"We'll see, then. And if you need my help, don't hesitate to call on me." Lorrimer rose, stifling a yawn. "Better be running along. I could do with a little more sleep." He shook hands with Corbin, picked up his black bag, and with Melhorn strode to the door.

ALONE, Corbin abruptly became aware of his own weariness. The library windows were bright with dawn, but a few hours of sleep would be welcome. When Melhorn came back into the room and suggested that they snatch a short rest, Corbin readily agreed.

It was well past noon when Corbin awoke. He had been looking forward to this day in particular. It was to have meant an entire day with Doris, and he was dismayed that so much of it had gone. He dressed hurriedly and descended to the lower floor.

At the foot of the stairs he met Nora Melhorn, who seemed to be on her way back to Doris' room. He asked eagerly, "Is Doris awake?"

"No, Jeffery." Her angular, patrician features were sallow from her long, sleepless vigil. "And I think it would be best not to wake her. Doris needs as much rest as she can get."

"Of course," Corbin said. Nora Melhorn continued on her way, and he sighed dismally. Then, with a fatalistic shrug of his shoulders, he went in search of the dining room.

The butler had breakfast waiting, or "brunch," to be more precise, Corbin thought. He helped himself, discovering that he was almost ravenously hungry. When he had finished, he lighted a cigarette and wandered out to the garden. Seated on a stone bench beneath an apple tree, he found Melhorn. The older man had a chess set laid out on the bench and seemed to be engaged in working out a problem. Corbin decided, as he approached, that Melhorn wasn't trying very hard.

They exchanged greetings and began a desultory conversation. Finally Melhorn suggested a game of chess, and Corbin agreed. He lost consistently, without being very much aware of the fact. His eyes kept wandering to the windows of Doris' room, partially visible from where he sat on the bench opposite Melhorn.

It wasn't until late afternoon that he learned Doris had at last awakened. Nora Melhorn consented to allowing him to spend a short time with the girl, cautioning him not to excite or alarm her.

DORIS was seated in bed. She looked refreshed and lovely, her features showing no traces of her experience early that morning. When Corbin had settled himself into a chair beside the bed, she laughed ruefully.

"I'm an awful pig, Jeff, sleeping so late. It must have been that Martini I drank last night."

Corbin's grin was teasing. "Oh, yeah? How do I know that was the only one you had?"

"But it was, Jeff. I really don't care for drinks—they make me sleepy."

"Well, what about that hypnotizing stunt our friend Dr. Amkeddar pulled you into? That might account for it." Corbin sat back in his chair, clasping his hands behind his head. He tried to look casual.

"Oh...that was nothing."

The grin faded from Corbin's lips. "You didn't seem to think so last night."

"Last night...?" Doris frowned a little and passed the back of one bandaged hand across her forehead. "It's funny, Jeff... I don't seem to remember what happened last night very well."

Corbin said through stiff lips, "You remember being hypnotized by Dr. Amkeddar?"

"Why, yes."

"And returning home?"

"Yes."

"Nothing after that?"

"No...nothing until I awoke a while ago." A faint alarm showed on Doris' face. "Jeff—is there anything wrong?"

"Of course not," Corbin said quickly. "I was just trying to help you decide why you slept so long." He hesitated a moment, then added, "You don't think that hypnotizing stunt of Dr. Amkeddar's might be responsible?"

"It couldn't be, Jeff. Amkeddar is all right."

Corbin gasped in consternation. "All right?"

Doris nodded with an eagerness almost child-like. "Certainly, Jeff. He wouldn't do anything wrong. I...I like him."

Corbin could only stare. A cold, terrible wind seemed to catch him and whirl him dizzily away and away.

Last night Doris had been afraid of Amkeddar. Now—she trusted him, liked him.

Corbin could see Amkeddar's plan now. The whole evil scheme was becoming clear. What, he wondered anxiously, would be the wily Indian's next move? After a moment he decided he knew, and dread was a constricting sensation in his chest.

Doris becoming more and more friendly with Amkeddar. Driving with him, dancing with him—visiting with him.

CHAPTER SEVEN
Top Man

CORBIN leaned toward the bed, his pretense of casualness abandoned. He said earnestly, "You didn't feel the same about Dr. Amkeddar last night. You told me you were afraid of him."

Doris' tawny eyes grew bewildered. She passed her hand across her forehead again, groping for memories that eluded her. Then she seemed to undergo a change. It was as though, in her search, she had found something that she hadn't known was there—something completely natural and logical, the obvious solution to her perplexity! She moved her slender shoulders in a shrug. She said, "A gal can change her mind, can't she?"

"There's no law against it, as far as I know," Corbin said. "But, Doris, have you stopped to consider whether you changed your mind of your own free will—or whether it was changed for you?"

"…I don't know what you're talking about." Her tone was cold, faintly hostile.

Corbin decided that he had to be more careful. He was treading dangerous ground—going counter to the new thoughts and emotions that Doris had been given. Wherever he touched upon her old attitude toward Amkeddar, her barriers would be up. He had to be careful—yet he wanted to see just how extensive those barriers were. He spoke softly, slowly.

"Doris, you remember being hypnotized by Dr. Amkeddar last night?"

"Of course."

"Well, hasn't it occurred to you that this might be responsible for your change of mind about him?"

"Don't be silly, Jeff. It was just an exhibition. There was really nothing more to it."

"But isn't it strange that you should experience such a complete and sudden change?"

"That's my own affair, Jeff."

Dismay flooded Corbin. Then came an overpowering anger that Amkeddar's stratagem should have been so successful. He threw further insinuations aside. For the moment he knew only that he had to fight this dangerous new attitude within Doris—had to fight it and conquer it.

He reached toward the bed and took one of the girl's hands. He fought to keep his voice steady.

"Doris, you've got to snap out of it. You aren't acting naturally, can't you understand that? You've been hypnotized—made to behave directly opposite to your true feelings. It's all part of a rotten scheme, and Dr. Amkeddar is behind it."

She drew her hand away. "Please, Jeff, don't be foolish. Dr. Amkeddar is…wonderful. He wouldn't do anything underhanded."

CORBIN persisted desperately, "The fact that you're talking like that shows he has. Look, Doris. Last night you disliked Amkeddar. You were actually afraid of him. And he knew it. He was interested in you, and didn't intend to leave matters as they were. I've no reason to be certain; but I think he suggested that parlor game to Mrs. Castleton, knowing that if he was able to hypnotize you, he could change your feelings toward him. And, Doris, that's just what he has done. The man's evil, I tell you—rotten clear through. If you don't snap out of it, he'll hurt you in some nasty twisted way."

Doris' tawny eyes flashed indignantly. "Jeffrey Corbin, I'll have you understand that I won't let you speak of Dr. Amkeddar like that. He…why, he's fine! You're just jealous."

Corbin sighed. He felt helpless, tired.

A discreet tapping sounded at the door. Doris called out an invitation to enter, and Melhorn strode into the room.

"Hope I'm not intruding."

"Of course not, Dad," Doris said pointedly. "I'm glad you came," She patted the bed. "Come on and sit down."

Melhorn settled himself gingerly. "Well, honey, how do you feel after that…uh…long sleep you had?"

"Swell."

"No bad dreams?"

"No…" She studied Melhorn's face, frowning. "Say, Dad, why does everyone ask so many questions? I'm not a sick child."

"Do they?" Melhorn threw a guarded glance at Corbin.

"Yes, definitely. First Aunt Nora, then Jeff, and now you."

"Well…" Clearly at a loss, Melhorn shrugged.

Corbin said, "Doris and I were discussing Dr. Amkeddar before you came in. She seems to think very highly of him."

Melhorn's grizzled brows rose sharply. "Very highly?"

"So it seems. I was trying to convince her that she didn't feel the same about him last night—before he hypnotized her. She refuses to believe me, or that the hypnosis could be responsible."

"It's just a lot of nonsense," Doris stated emphatically.

Melhorn rose slowly to his feet. "See here, Doris, suppose I told you that it wasn't a lot of nonsense—that Jeff was perfectly right?"

"I still won't believe it."

"But good heavens, girl, doesn't my word mean anything? Jeff's right. I know he's right!"

Doris turned her face away. "Please, Dad. Why lie to me? I know my own feelings."

Melhorn made a coughing sound. His face looked perplexed. He leaned over the bed and grasped her shoulders with earnest intensity.

"Doris—have I ever lied to you? About anything?"

"…No."

"Then why should I be lying now?"

"I don't know. Oh—I don't know!" Her voice rose with a shrill note of agitation. "Please leave me alone… Why does everyone keep asking me questions—hounding me? I can't help the way I feel. I like Dr. Amkeddar. I've always liked him. Nothing you can say will change that." She twisted from Melhorn's grasp and buried her face in the pillow. Her body shook with sobs.

Melhorn straightened slowly. He seemed burned out, defeated—suddenly old.

THE door abruptly opened and Nora Melhorn came into the room. With a swift, appraising glance at the distraught girl in the bed, she turned indignantly on Melhorn and Corbin.

"Didn't I tell you not to excite her? She's in no condition to be asked a lot of questions. Now go on out of here, both of you. She'll be a nervous wreck if she isn't left in peace."

Melhorn looked in weary resignation at Corbin, turned, and led the way from the room. In the library he poured drinks. His hands shook a little, Corbin noticed. The observation was made with sympathy and understanding. Corbin felt anything but steady himself.

The drinks turned out to be stiff ones, and straight, which suited Corbin perfectly. He needed something to fill the cold hollow inside him.

"What on earth do you make of it, Jeff?" Melhorn asked after a moment. "Doris seems to have developed what might almost be called a crush on our friend Amkeddar."

"Exactly," Corbin said. "But developed hardly describes it. We might say it was cut to size and nailed on."

"Hypnotism, eh?"

"I'm not so sure. It may go deeper than that. Remember the hypodermic mark on her arm that Lorrimer told us about."

Melhorn nodded slowly. "And those other people he mentioned, with identical marks—do you suppose the same thing happened to them?"

"I don't know. It doesn't seem likely that Amkeddar would go in for that sort of thing on a grand scale. I'd say that most of the people he has a hold on were ready, willing, and able."

"Most?"

"Well, a few may have had to be...persuaded."

"But how does that account for the fact that all have hypodermic marks?"

Corbin spread his hands. "Identical hypodermic marks don't necessarily mean identical drugs, with identical effects," he pointed out.

"That's right, of course," Melhorn agreed.

Corbin went on, "As a theory, we might say that some degree of hypnotism accompanied all injections, but the different drugs used produced different results. As to what those results are, I...I don't know." Corbin stared at his glass, wondering if Melhorn had detected the evasion. He was more than fairly certain that he did know.

There was a momentary silence. Melhorn nibbled thoughtfully at his lip. Finally he said, "Ummm...Jeff, those results you spoke of—you don't suppose that tigers are somehow involved?"

Corbin pretended surprise. "Tigers? What do you mean?"

MELHORN looked hesitant. "Well, tigers seem to be a thread running through this whole fantastic business. There are the tiger tracks we found in the garden. If, as you say, Jeff, they were made at the same time as Doris', the fact that it didn't attack her shows that it was definitely an unusual animal. And if its purpose actually had been to lead her somewhere, it would seem to have qualities almost...well, human.

"Then there is the tiger we saw leaving Amkeddar's estate. The hypodermic mark in Doris' arm, her strange and sudden affection for Amkeddar, all show that he is involved. Therefore, she must have been somewhere on his premises—

most likely in that laboratory of his—at the same time as us. And she returned home shortly before we did. But, Jeff, the only living thing that left Amkeddar's place was that tiger we saw.

"And finally there is the insinuation you mentioned, made by Mrs. Castleton's gateman. The possibility that some people might be tigers." Melhorn studied his hands as though abruptly self-conscious. "Dash it, Jeff! Can't you see what it all adds up to?"

Corbin nodded slowly. "I've known for quite a while. I hesitated to come right out with it, though, because I saw how upset you were over Doris, and I was afraid that this inference would be a knockout blow. I had a hard enough time hanging on to my own reason."

Melhorn's face twisted. He flung out his hands in a gesture of bewilderment and demanded, "What on earth could that devil be up to? What is the reason behind everything?"

"Where the tigers are concerned, I don't know," Corbin said. "But as it pertains to Doris, the whole affair seems clear enough. Amkeddar was interested in her, but he saw that she disliked and feared him. The most effective way of getting around these feelings was for him to use his talent for hypnosis. Most likely he suggested that parlor game to Mrs. Castleton, knowing it would sooner or later give him his chance. It did. He planted in Doris' mind the post-hypnotic suggestion that she was later to come to his estate. There he put the finishing touches to his rotten scheme. Doris is now convinced that she has always liked and trusted him, and she seems to have been coached so thoroughly that she just won't listen to what anyone has to say to the contrary.

"And now, of course, Amkeddar can see her as often as he wants to, and he doesn't have to be secretive about it. If anyone objects, what good will it do? Doris is convinced that she likes him. She's of legal age, quite free to choose her own friends. He can take her out—and nobody will be the wiser. It's common knowledge that women find him romantic and fascinating. Why should Doris be any different? The fact that she feels that way won't be considered unusual at all."

Melhorn's features were set in stern lines. He said grimly, "I certainly won't permit Doris to see that scoundrel!"

"But what can you do to stop her?" Corbin asked gently. "Would you take the stand of most parents—order her from the house? That would be playing directly into Amkeddar's hands. And of course there's the fact that Doris isn't responsible for her condition."

MELHORN slumped in defeated silence. He worried at his lip, eyes dark with inner turmoil.

Corbin said, "This isn't easy for me either. The way I feel about Doris should be obvious enough. It's taking everything I've got to keep from blowing my top. But we'll have to have clear heads if we're to spoil Amkeddar's little game."

Melhorn gestured despairingly. "Yes—but how?"

"Amkeddar himself may show us a way. He has the ball right now, but sooner or later he'll fumble it. In the meantime, Doris has to be kept out of his reach. Lorrimer can help us in doing that. He can give Doris sedatives or something of the sort to keep her in bed."

Melhorn nodded eagerly. "That's an idea, Jeff. We'll try it."

Evening soon came. After a somewhat silent dinner with Melhorn, Corbin announced his intention of returning to the city.

"This has been a sorry weekend for you, Jeff," Melhorn said. "But the invitation still stands. In fact, it's now obligatory, and a special favor to me, considering what has happened. I'll be looking for you next week."

"I'll be here," Corbin responded. "Be sure to let me know if anything comes up in the meantime." He shook hands with Melhorn, then went to bid farewell to Doris. She offered her hand to him coolly.

"Goodnight, Jeff."

"I'll be back next week, Doris."

"Will you?" She didn't seem interested.

Corbin left, an ache nagging in his chest. Determination to fight Amkeddar surged through him with renewed force. But he wondered if, despite his efforts, the Doris of old would ever be restored to him.

CHAPTER EIGHT
Watch By Night

THE severe, scholarly-looking woman who served as Corbin's secretary entered the office with an air of mild excitement. She said, "Mr. Barton Melhorn wishes to see you. He says it is important."

Corbin laid aside his pen, thoughts flaring anxiously. Melhorn's visit could only concern Doris, he knew. Only a few days had passed since his tumultuous weekend visit to Sylvan Heights. Could something have happened so soon?

Corbin rose from the desk. "Send Mr. Melhorn in at once."

Melhorn's face was drawn, his eyes shadowed with worry. He shook Corbin's hand briefly and dropped into a chair. He spoke without preamble.

"Amkeddar seems to have taken another move in the game, Jeff."

"How do you mean?" Corbin asked tensely. "What has he done?"

"I don't know what he's done, Jeff. But Doris…strayed again last night. I knew nothing about it until Nora told me this morning. She'd brought Doris breakfast as usual and found Doris' hands and feet scratched and muddy like…like the first time."

Corbin fought down a surge of angry dismay. "But Lorrimer? Didn't he give her something to keep her in bed?"

Melhorn nodded. "He did. It seems, however, that Amkeddar's control over Doris is stronger. The mind frequently can claim strange victories over the body, you know. And besides, there's hypnotism and Lord knows what else mixed up in it."

"That washes up my little scheme for keeping Doris away from Amkeddar," Corbin mused bleakly. "Sedatives aren't strong enough. We could try narcotics—dope, to be exact. But that would be too much like fighting fire with atomic bombs."

Melhorn sighed tiredly. "Then we're licked, isn't that it? For Amkeddar to have acted so soon can only mean he suspected there was little or nothing we could do against him. Now he knows. Obviously, he sent for Doris to question her."

"And now he can go ahead with the rest of his rotten plan—whatever it is." Corbin's voice was leaden.

"There's one possibility left," Melhorn said after a momentary silence. "We could go to the police."

"That wouldn't do any good. Amkeddar would simply deny anything we tried to pin on him—and Doris would back him up."

"But we can't just sit back and do nothing at all, Jeff! Amkeddar now knows he has a clear path for whatever deviltry he has in mind. He must be stopped before it's too late."

CORBIN fell to pacing the floor, reddish brows pinched together in an agony of thought. Finally, eyes glittering, he whirled to a stop before Melhorn. "If I'm not wrong about one angle of this business, we still have a hand to play. As I said before, it's Amkeddar's move. Well, he's made that move. He's shown us a way to get at him."

"But I don't see how…" Melhorn looked puzzled.

"He's shown us a way—by sending for Doris. Don't you see? There's a good chance that he may send for her again—and soon. If and when he does, I'm going to follow her. Most likely she'll go directly to his estate, as seems the usual procedure. I'll slip inside somehow. Amkeddar will hardly expect anything like that, and with luck I can take him by surprise. If I can…" Corbin's lips thinned in a hard smile. "…our troubles are over. I'll persuade him at gunpoint to release Doris from his control. He'll never get another chance at her after that. We'll be on guard against him, and once more in possession of her own will, Doris will cooperate with us."

"You'll be taking a terrible risk, Jeff," Melhorn pointed out. "If you should be caught—"

"Devil the risk!" Corbin grunted. "It's Doris I'm worried about."

Melhorn shook his head slowly. "Amkeddar's an utter rogue, Jeff. If you fall into his hands a second time, you won't get off as lightly as before. We must be prepared for that emergency. I'll agree to your plan only if you let me go along. I could wait outside, in the car, and if there is any indication that something has happened to you, I could get the police before Amkeddar has time to do anything drastic."

Corbin grinned slightly and shrugged. "Have it your own way, then. I'll settle my affairs here and drive out to Sylvan Heights this evening. Then, each night, we'll watch the windows of Doris' room. When she leaves, we'll follow. But remember—not a word of this to Doris. Amkeddar may question her and be warned."

"As you say, Jeff." Melhorn rose and gripped Corbin's hand. "I'll arrange to have you slipped secretly into the house when you arrive. In the meantime, I'd better be getting back."

The expression confidence faded from Corbin's face as Melhorn left. Realization struck into him of how completely foolhardy was his plan. What he intended to do was equivalent to bearding the lion—or more appropriately, the tiger—in its den. Yet it seemed to be the only course against Amkeddar open to him. There could be no misgivings or regrets.

PALE silver radiance from a moon near full etched the house and grounds in somber shades of black and gray. A thin wind moved like a fretful ghost among the leaves of trees and shrubs. To Corbin, crouching with Melhorn behind a screen of rhododendron bushes, the rustling of the foliage seemed whispers of menace. Long minutes of peering through the darkness made the moon-cast shadows appear to flow and undulate, as though possessed of inimical alien life.

With a twinge of self-disgust, Corbin altered the direction of his thoughts. He was beginning to image things. He and Melhorn had been watching for several hours now, and this was the third night of their vigil. The strain, Corbin decided, was beginning to tell.

He shifted impatiently, dimly aware that Melhorn stirred also. He whispered, "Wish something would happen. This waiting is getting on my nerves."

"Maybe we were wrong, Jeff," Melhorn whispered in return. "Maybe Amkeddar doesn't intend to send for Doris after all. Not for a long time, anyway."

"Or maybe Doris found out I was here, and realized what we were up to."

"I hardly think so. We were too careful about that end."

"Hope you're right." Corbin settled into a more comfortable position on the damp turf and returned his attention to the house. It stood some thirty feet away, bulking grayly in the moonlit dusk. The French windows of Doris' room, slightly opened, were clearly visible over the top of the terrace balustrade. With the moonlight flooding the terrace and gleaming on the windowpanes, no movement could possibly be missed.

Corbin had chosen his and Melhorn's vantage point carefully. It was located amid the dense shrubbery at the base of the two-story garage, where by night shadows were thickest. From here the entire garden and rear of the house could most easily be seen, the garage wall itself forming a protection against any possibility of attack from behind. And from the garage, the driveway led down to the road in front of the house. Corbin's roadster stood on the driveway, ready for immediate use.

THE long minutes dragged slowly past. Despite himself, Corbin had almost dozed off when abruptly he felt the grip of Melhorn's finger's upon his arm. Full awareness flowed back to him with a rush. Glancing instinctively at the windows of Doris' room, he saw instantly what had alerted Melhorn. The windows were moving—opening!

Corbin held his breath tautly. The event for which he had so long and impatiently been waiting was actually taking place at last. Or—was it merely some chance vagary of the wind that was swinging the windows wide? He watched in mounting tenseness as the opening in the window grew.

Then, through the opening, the head and shoulders of a girl—all that was visible over the top of the terrace balustrade—moved into sight. It was Doris, pale and wraith-like in the silver radiance of the moon. She was staring straight before her as though intent upon something in the far distance. A long moment she stood there, and then she suddenly bent, moving out of sight behind the balustrade. She might have reached down to pick up something at her feet. But she did not straighten up into view again.

Corbin squinted in perplexity. What was Doris doing? Had she—fainted? In another instant, as he watched, a little tawny shape leaped to the top of the balustrade, poised there a moment, and jumped to the ground below. An animal—a tiger! And the soft thud of its contact with the turf showed that it was real, not a hallucination brought on by overwrought nerves.

SHRUBBERY at the bottom of the terrace momentarily hid the creature from view. Then, with a silence almost uncanny, it padded out onto the moonlit lawn. It paused a moment, swinging its sleek head about as though in quest of an objective or of prey. Some obscure decision was reached. Like a tawny ghost, the tiger trotted toward the driveway and disappeared in the direction of the road.

Melhorn sucked in breath with a rasping noise. "Jeff— that tiger—could it possibly have been—?"

"That's what I'm going to find out," Corbin said metallically. He rose, ran toward the terrace, and climbed over the balustrade. At the threshold of the French windows lay a softly gleaming heap of cloth. He picked the material up and shook it out. A nightgown. Doris' nightgown, obviously. He let it drop back to the floor and went into the room. The bed had been slept in, but now was empty. A short search showed that, except for himself, the room was devoid of any occupant.

The incredible conclusion, then, was inescapable. The tiger he and Melhorn had seen...had been Doris.

Corbin joined Melhorn on the lawn. He nodded in answer to the question on the older man's face. "Doris and the tiger were one and the same, all right. If it hadn't happened before, I'd say it was impossible—downright ridiculous." He shrugged slightly, and his tone hardened. "As incredible and unbelievable as all this seems to be, Barton, my plan seems to be working out. A tiger moves too fast to follow, but there's only one place to which it...she...can be going—Amkeddar's estate. Traveling in my car, we should reach there around the same time."

With a gesture, he turned and went swiftly to the roadster in the driveway. When Melhorn had climbed in beside him, he sent the car roaring toward the road with a clash of gears.

CHAPTER NINE
Rites of the Tiger

CEDAR Road was a pale gray ribbon under the moon, unwinding through the night-steeped countryside. Corbin drove without lights, hunched over the steering wheel, eyes bleakly intent.

A cool wind whipped past the speeding roadster. It carried the mingled scents of grass and leaves and moist earth. Crickets chirped in the dark fields on either side of the road. Overhead the stars glittered in all their countless multitudes, like jewels adorning the black velvet tapestry of the sky.

Corbin felt a brief surge of nostalgia. It was a night, he thought, for life and hope. It was a night, too, for defeat and death.

He gripped the steering wheel tighter, and his lips thinned with pressure—he wasn't going to think about that.

Presently a familiar stone wall appeared down the road a ways, a leprous gray in the moonlight. Using the forward momentum of the car, Corbin coasted to within some fifty yards or so of the enclosure. Then he turned off the road, stopping behind a concealing fringe of bushes. He and Melhorn left the car quickly and moved to a spot at the edge of the road from where they could watch the gate.

"I hope Dor—the tiger didn't get here ahead of us," Melhorn whispered after a moment.

Corbin shook his head. "I drove fast enough to beat anything on legs, even allowing for short cuts…" About to speak again, he checked himself abruptly and nudged Melhorn's arm.

A tiger was trotting up from the other end of the road. It stopped at the gate. Inserting its muzzle between the bars, it growled softly. After a moment a metallic clicking sounded, followed by the squeal of hinges as the gate swung open. The tiger disappeared inside the wall, and the gate squealed and clicked shut.

Corbin's face was set grimly. "It seems we got here first after all. Well, this is it. Now to see if I can put an end to Amkeddar's little game." He started to straighten up, intending to approach and climb the wall. The next instant he froze into startled rigidity.

A *second* tiger was crossing the road directly before the gate, stopping when it had reached the barrier. It, too, growled softly. Again the gate swung open and shut.

CORBIN and Melhorn stared at each other in bewilderment. Corbin whispered, "That throws a monkey wrench into the works. The question now is—which of those two tigers was Doris? My plan might all too easily go haywire on that point."

"Looking at it the other way around, Jeff," Melhorn put in, "who was the second tiger? Amkeddar?"

"That might be a good guess."

"What are you going to do now, Jeff?"

Corbin considered, frowning anxiously. "I'm going to watch a while longer. I have an idea about the appearance of that second tiger."

They settled themselves once more. Long minutes passed. Then, padding almost noiselessly past their hiding place, came a third tiger! This latest arrival also stopped at the gate and was admitted.

Melhorn glanced in startled questioning at Corbin. "Is that what you were waiting for?"

Corbin nodded, eyes sweeping the road watchfully. "I was acting on the old adage that where there's smoke, there's fire. A second tiger could have meant the appearance of more—and did. Notice how what we've seen ties in with the rumor about tigers roaming Sylvan Heights at night? Only they don't roam—they have a definite destination."

Melhorn breathed sharply. "And the visitors Amkeddar receives late at night, Jeff! And…and the hypodermic marks in the arms of Doris and the others Lorrimer told us about. It all fits. As we suspected, the hypodermic marks indicate a drug that gives the ability to…to change. For certain reasons—of which convenience in reaching him may be one—Amkeddar is giving his visitors this ability."

"Or giving it to them as they gradually become established members of his…clientele," Corbin added. Abruptly he raised his hand in a gesture of warning. A fourth tiger had appeared up the road and was trotting quickly toward the gate.

Eyes narrowed and intent, Corbin continued to watch. Within the next ten minutes over a dozen more arrived. Then came a long interval during which there were no further appearances. From beyond the wall girdling Amkeddar's estate, a faint quick throbbing became audible. It was sustained, compelling, with a swift insistent tempo that caught at the pulses.

Phrr-o-o-oom, br-r-um, br-r-um, br-r-um; phrr-o-o-oom, br-r-um, br-r-um, br-r-um!

CORBIN'S eyes widened startledly. Drums! Drums, muffled by intervening walls, but obviously nearby, beating out a barbaric intoxicating rhythm. Visions of a ceremonial fire deep in a night-wrapped jungle, of weirdly costumed savages dancing in homage to a pagan god, momentarily flitted through Corbin's mind.

Melhorn touched Corbin's arm, features twisted in a sort of incredulous perplexity. "Drums, Jeff! What in the world can be going on in there?"

"That's what I intend to find out," Corbin rose purposefully to his feet.

"...You mean you're still going inside?"

"Yes. My original plan was spoiled by that wild animal tamer's nightmare we saw parading through the gate. But something's going on—something important. If I can learn just what, the information may be even more effective against Amkeddar than what I first intended to do. We've waited long enough to be certain that no more tigers will arrive. Besides, I suspect those drums wouldn't have started unless everybody was present."

Melhorn nodded slowly. "All right, Jeff—and be careful. I'll stay here and listen. If I hear anything that indicates you've been caught, I'll rush straight to the police."

Corbin lifted a hand in farewell and began moving toward the wall, threading his way carefully through the tangle of weeds and shrubs. The steady throbbing of the drums was like a growled threat in his ears. He touched the revolver that he carried in a pocket of his dark coat, and his jaw muscles tightened.

Shortly the wall loomed up before him. As he had noticed earlier, it was covered with cracks and overgrown with vines. Climbing over would be easy enough. He chose what seemed an especially suitable place and started up.

Reaching the top, he paused to examine the scene below. The house was dark and lifeless. Light, however, shone behind the small barred windows set high in the walls of the laboratory building. The drumming, somewhat louder now, seemed to be issuing from here. As Corbin listened, another sound became audible—the high thin eerie wailing of flutes, rising and falling in time to the swift tempo of the drums. There was something wild and primeval about the music—if music it was—that tugged insistently at long-buried instincts. Corbin felt an insidious urge to seek and kill, to tear at warm quivering flesh, to revel in the scent and taste of fresh hot blood. He shuddered, forcing himself to ignore the music and concentrate on the task at hand.

THE grounds surrounding the house and laboratory still had their untended jungle-like appearance. Carefully, Corbin probed the shadows, searching for guards. A movement in the wilderness of tangled shrubbery caught his eye. He flattened himself against the top of the wall, senses leaping in sudden alarm.

A dark shape moved into a pool of moonlight. Above the weird rhythm of drums and flutes sounded a deep terrified lowing, Corbin's eyes narrowed in astonishment. A cow! Untethered, free to wander about at will, a cow was roaming the grounds.

Nor was it the only one. As Corbin stared, he saw what must have been quite a large number of cows moving restlessly, as though in frightened seeking of escape, about the enclosure. And there were smaller shapes, lighter in color, that could only have been sheep.

He frowned in perplexity. What did the presence of these animals mean? Did it have some connection with the strange gathering in Amkeddar's laboratory?

He intended to find out. If there were guards, they would have difficulty in discovering an intruder among the constantly shifting animals. Reaching the laboratory would present less danger than he had expected.

Corbin squirmed around to the inner side of the wall, lowered his legs over the edge, and with the aid of vines and cracks began to descend. When he had reached the ground, he crouched tensely, listening. There was no movement save that of the animals, no sound above the beat of drums and the wail of flutes save an occasional plaintive cry of a cow or sheep.

Moving from tree to tree and bush to bush like a hunter stalking game, Corbin began to move toward the laboratory. Now a new sound rose, deep-throated growls and snarls, muffled by building walls, that could only have been made by tigers.

Corbin reached the edge of the gravel driveway and stopped for a moment behind a concealing mass of shrubbery. Nearby, at the end of the driveway, loomed the house. Almost directly across from him was the laboratory, alive and menacing with the strange sounds inside it. Still he saw no guards. Listening to the music and the vocalized blood lust of the tigers, aware of the terror-driven animals wandering the grounds about him, he began to understand why. The tigers were being incited by the music to a killing frenzy. And if the presence of the cows and sheep outside meant that the tigers were to be released, to attack, it would hardly be safe for a guard—or any other human—to be in the way.

THERE was danger after all, Corbin realized sharply. He had to find some means of shelter before the tigers were loosed. He considered the idea in dismay. It would interfere with his plan to spy on the proceedings in the laboratory.

Perhaps if he were quick—Corbin wasted no further time in taking precautions against discovery. Emerging from behind the shrubbery, he darted quickly across the driveway, reached the deep shadows at the base of the laboratory wall nearest the house.

A solution to his problem presented itself unexpectedly. Towering up beside the wall, close by, was a large tree. He traced the pattern of its outflung boughs and found that one stretched directly beneath a window of the laboratory. Action followed thought automatically. Corbin reached the tree in two quick strides and began to pull himself up.

Gaining the bough he had marked for use, he carefully inched along its length, moving toward the window. The bough was not as thick as he'd hoped it would be, and it bent in creaking protest under his weight. Several times he expected it to break loose and send him plunging to the ground. But it held, and at last he reached the window. Grasping the bars that covered it, he peered eagerly through.

The scene upon which he centered his eyes was like a nightmare or a delusion of a drug-crazed mind made real. The light that filled the interior of the building Amkeddar called his laboratory came from a number of open braziers, suspended from tripod supports, placed about the walls of the room. Grotesque shadows leaped and danced as the flames within the braziers rose and fell, flickered and writhed. At the far end of the single huge chamber, against a wall covered with a great crimson tapestry upon which was emblazoned in gold the figure of a rampant tiger, was a raised dais crowned by two ornate throne-like chairs. Amkeddar sat in one of the chairs, garbed in a black robe and turban, a smile of sly satisfaction curving his thin lips, a faint mockery glittering in his sleepily lidded jet eyes. In the other chair was—Doris!

Corbin felt an over-mastering surge of anger as he looked at her. Hate for Amkeddar became a thing verging on the brink of madness.

DORIS was clad only in a brief skirt and halter affair fashioned from a tiger skin, her bare arms and legs gleaming whitely in the light from the flaming braziers. She was decked barbarically in a profusion of jeweled ornaments. A headdress that was the preserved upper half of a tiger's head covered her copper-brown hair, which, unbound, hung in thick curls about her slender shoulders. She was staring rigidly before her, features set and immobile like a carving in perfect semblance of life.

Several feet beyond the dais was a huge stone block. A woman lay upon the block, bound by chains fastened to rings in the stone, her frantically writhing brown form naked, her long black hair matted and disheveled by her futile struggles to break free. It was Kumara. And typical of what Corbin already knew of the Indian woman's character, there was no fear or terror on her face, only a withering hatred for Amkeddar, a cold steely desperation at her plight.

Corbin suddenly realized that the stone block was an altar. Deep channels grooved its top as though to permit liquid to run off into the low shallow trough running around the base. Corbin thought he knew what that liquid was—blood!

Kumara evidently was to be a sacrifice in some hellish rite, which even now was reaching its grim climax.

For circling the block, nose to tail, moving to the eerie music in a continuous parade, went almost a score of tigers. Around and around they padded, in a queer jiggling swaying dance, red tongues lolling and slavering, tawny eyes blazing. With growing frequency, the dancers were glancing up at the figure imprisoned on the top of the block. Corbin heard the increasing volume of their growls, impatient, demanding.

The drums pounded louder, the flutes wailed higher, as the music scaled new heights of barbaric frenzy. Despite himself, Corbin felt his pulses race and throb. Again he experienced a sly but compelling urge to seek and kill. He fought it down in a search for the source of the enthralling rhythm. It came, he discovered shortly, from a group of four Indians squatting together to the right of the dais, almost beyond his field of vision. They were stripped to the waist, brown skins glistening with sweat from their efforts.

Finally Amkeddar rose to his feet, tall and satanic in his black garments. A lifted hand brought immediate silence from the musicians. The tigers ceased their dance, to sit in an eager waiting ring about the stone block. At a gesture from Amkeddar, Doris slowly stood up, paganly lovely in her scanty tiger skins and jeweled ornaments.

From his black robe, Amkeddar pulled a long wickedly shining knife. He extended this to Doris with a few curtly spoken words. She took the knife. Gold-flecked eyes unblinking, face expressionless as an ivory mask, she moved like an automaton to the stone block, poised the blade over Kumara's heart.

AMKEDDAR raised his hand again. All those in the room seemed to be waiting. There was a deep silence, an utter lack of motion, which made the tableau weirdly unreal.

An icy current rushed through Corbin's veins. When Amkeddar's hand came down, he knew, the music would start up again, wilder and swifter than before. Doris' knife would flash down, and the tigers, inflamed to madness by the smell and taste of blood, would rush out into the night, to rend and tear insensately at the cattle and sheep wandering about the grounds.

This latter event was unimportant. But what Doris was going to do in another instant was...*murder!* Her entire bearing testified that she was herself a helpless victim of circumstance, an enslaved unwilling dupe; yet the fact of the impending crime remained.

And Kumara—Corbin was in little doubt as to his feelings toward the Indian woman. For her he knew an initial feeling of respect, admiration, even liking. He couldn't sit by idly and watch her die. And above all, Doris had to be saved from the ghastly deed she was shortly to commit.

But—what could he do? There was no way he could stop the proceedings without betraying his presence. Capture quite likely would mean that he, too, would become a victim of sacrifice.

Corbin shifted his body in an agony of desperation. There was a sudden snapping noise, piercing like a thunderclap into the deep silence. He found himself plummeting to the ground, to strike with a numbing thud even before the dismaying realization of what had happened formed completely in his mind.

The bough upon which he had been perched had broken under the pressure of his weight!

From within the laboratory came a medley of startled growls and shouts. The alarm had been given. The presence of a lurker outside was now known. Pursuit—and possibly capture—would swiftly follow.

CHAPTER TEN
A Nocturnal Visit

ANXIETY swept Corbin like a sudden gale, tearing away the fog that filled his dazed mind. If the fall had crippled him...

Impelled by a frantic sense of dread, he sat up, moving his limbs experimentally. Relief came. There were no sprains or broken bones. He had merely been bruised by his drop, briefly stunned.

From within the building came the pounding of feet and the excited snarls of tigers. Urgency flashed through Corbin. He pulled himself erect and began to run toward the wall, stiffly and clumsily at first, then with increasing limberness. Behind him, he heard a door flung open. A sudden flood of light poured over him, throwing his shadow with grotesque effect on the shrubbery before him and on the wall ahead. A roar of wild confusion enveloped the enclosure as the cattle and sheep, previously uneasy, plunged about in blind panic under the abrupt onslaught of light, noise, and the smell of tigers released by the opened door. Corbin twice narrowly escaped being trampled.

Above the terrified cries of cattle and sheep and the eager growls of tigers lifted a human voice.

"There he is! After him, you fools! Don't let him get away!"

Corbin darted a glance in his rear. Amkeddar stood framed in the light from the doorway, gesturing furiously at the four Indians. Another glance an instant later showed the entire group of five rushing forward in pursuit.

Desperately Corbin increased his already mad pace. The wall was close, but climbing it would take time. The others might reach him before he had gained the top.

And then he tripped as one of his pistoning feet caught in a tangle of weeds, fell sprawling. Shouts of triumph rose in unison from Amkeddar and his henchmen.

Clawing wildly to his feet, Corbin measured in dismay the distance to the wall remaining. He'd never make it now. His fall had cost him what little lead he'd had. The only thing left to do was stand and fight it out.

Abruptly he recalled something important—the revolver! Unaccustomed to carrying weapons, he'd almost forgotten about it. Consternation rushed over him in an icy deluge, however, when he reached into the pocket where he had placed the gun. It was gone! With a sick, empty feeling, he realized it had evidently been shaken from his pocket during one of his two falls.

HE SET his lips whitely. He'd have to give battle with his bare hands, then. And at odds of five to one, there could be only one result. He thought wanly of Melhorn. There was little doubt that Melhorn had already been warned and would return presently with the police. But Corbin was grimly certain that he would no longer be alive when they came.

In another moment, and from a totally unexpected quarter, came an interruption, which to Corbin meant all the difference between life and death.

The tigers within the building had been goaded to a killing frenzy by the effluvium of terror and of delectable warm flesh given off by the cattle and sheep milling about in chaos on the grounds. Up to this point, some understanding with, or command from, Amkeddar had kept them inside. But now, unable to resist any longer instincts and lusts that drew them as surely and inexorably as the Moon draws tides, they erupted through the doorway in a tawny wave. Snarling in bloodthirsty ferocity, they threw themselves upon the terrified animals within the enclosure, tearing and slashing in savage abandon.

Corbin was vividly aware that the tigers presented a new and even greater danger. In their utterly berserk condition, they would stop at nothing. To get in the way of any one of them would be sheer suicide.

Amkeddar and his cohorts apparently realized this. The sudden appearance of the tigers froze them in their tracks. And then, as the carnage began in all its indescribable uproar and violence, the four Indians scattered in terror. Amkeddar alone stood his ground, glaring baffledly from Corbin to the pandemonium around him. He seemed torn between his desire to flee and his reluctance to let Corbin escape.

The opportunity was too good to miss. Corbin whirled and ran the remaining distance to the wall. Hurling himself desperately at the blanketing vines, he began to scramble up.

Once he glanced back. The flood of light pouring from the doorway of the building behind showed Amkeddar bent on all fours, huddling strangely in his black robes. In the next instant a tiger emerged from beneath the swathing garments. Its blazing eyes settled vindictively on Corbin. Then, as though released from a catapult, it sprang forward, bounding in great leaps toward the wall.

FRANTICALLY, Corbin hauled himself up the few feet separating him from the top. He was none too soon. The tiger's taloned forepaws clutched futilely at the place where his legs had been an instant before.

A raging feline demon, the tiger fell back to the ground. It did not give up the chase immediately, however. It launched itself once more at the wall and sought to clamber up by digging its talons into the vines. But the rope-like strands of vegetation broke under the tiger's weight and the sharpness of its claws. Again it fell back, snarling in impotent rage.

By this time Corbin had swung himself around the top of the wall and was lowering himself down the other side. Dropping the few feet to the ground that remained, he set out at a run toward the spot where he had left Melhorn and the roadster.

The roar of a car motor rose abruptly above the tumult beyond the wall. Corbin felt a wrench of dismay. Alarmed by the bedlam, Melhorn was starting out for the police. If Corbin were left behind, afoot and unarmed...

Corbin knew the wall was only a temporary obstacle. Amkeddar wouldn't give up easily. Even now, in his tiger's body, he must be racing toward the gate.

In desperation Corbin whipped himself to greater speed. He saw the car in the moonlight, moving toward the road. With his last reserves of strength, he released a shout.

"Wait! Here I am! It's Jeff!"

The sudden grinding of brakes was like music to Corbin. He reached the car and tumbled in without bothering to open the door.

"Let's go!" he gasped. "And fast!

A glance at Corbin's strained, haggard features galvanized Melhorn into motion. He jerked the roadster into gear, stamped down on the accelerator. At ever-increasing speed, they shot down the road, toward the highway.

The frightful cacophony of animal growls and screams from behind the wall faded into the distance and finally died. There was only the muted roar of the car engine, the whir of tires on concrete, and the soothing trill of crickets in the night-shrouded fields.

Slowly the tension drained from Corbin's aching body. He relaxed in his seat, breathing deeply of the cool air that streamed past. For his thoughts, however, there was no respite. Darkly, grimly, he was aware that his deadly contest with Amkeddar was far from being over. Though not exactly a prisoner in the enemy camp, Doris was still a helpless captive, bound by an evil influence more effective than chains. In that respect, the score remained in Amkeddar's favor.

CORBIN found a shred of comfort in the fact that his efforts hadn't been entirely without profit. He knew now what went on within the walls of Amkeddar's estate. And he had at once prevented Doris from being used as an unwitting tool for murder and gained a reprieve for Kumara, the intended victim. Amkeddar's vicious ceremony had been so completely disrupted that there was little if any possibility of his starting all over this night.

They reached the main highway. Melhorn turned into it, only then slackening the roadster's meteoric pace. After a moment he spoke.

"What in the world was that racket back there all about, Jeff? What happened?"

Tersely Corbin explained. He told of climbing the tree, and of what he had seen taking place inside the building which was supposed to be Amkeddar's laboratory. Then he detailed the sequence of events following the alarm given by his unexpected plunge to the ground and culminating in his return to the car.

He went on, "A number of things are now clear. Amkeddar's research work is just a blind. What he's actually doing is running some fantastic sort of cult, giving its members the ability to change from human to tiger form. The animals he buys, apparently for his experiments, are really used as victims in orgies of killing. And it's all decked out in fancy trimmings, from a sacrificial ceremony that excites the tiger congregation to the proper pitch of bloodthirstiness, to outdoor surroundings that have an appropriately jungle-like atmosphere.

"We already know that Amkeddar's converts are wealthy residents of Sylvan Heights. There are the rumors you mentioned about Amkeddar's receiving visits late at night from wealthy women—rumors that have a sound basis in fact when you consider that they were in all probability circulated by the chauffeurs who in the beginning drove these women to Amkeddar's place. There are the hypodermic marks in the arms of numerous wealthy persons that Lorrimer told us about, marks the same as those borne by Doris. And there is the strange reluctance of numerous wealthy persons, also noted by Lorrimer, to discuss tigers in any manner or form. This reluctance is understandable enough, considering that these persons most likely are members of Amkeddar's cult and have the ability to change into tigers.

"And finally—why are people of this class, drawn to Amkeddar?" Corbin nodded at Melhorn. "You supplied that explanation. It's because they are of the amoral, bored type, with too much money and too much time, who jump at anything that offers novelty—particularly in the way of strange and unusual thrills. With his cult, Amkeddar is supplying this kind of entertainment. It beats a nightclub hollow. And you can bet it's expensive. Amkeddar's cultists are undoubtedly paying through the nose for their fun—with blackmail or extortion through hypnotism staring them in the face if they try to back out.

"But—is money the motive for Amkeddar's cult? I don't think so. It doesn't agree with what I've pieced together of Amkeddar's character. He's the sort who plays for the highest possible stakes. Money is a necessity, but only a minor factor. What he's after is something else—something that would make me lose a lot of sleep if I knew what it was."

MELHORN drove in thoughtful silence. Peering about him, Corbin saw that they were near the house.

Abruptly Melhorn asked, "What about the Indian woman—Kumara? Why should Amkeddar want her killed as a sacrifice?"

"To get rid of her, obviously," Corbin said. "The sacrifice part was just a lot of mumbo-jumbo intended to gloss over the fact of it being outright murder. Amkeddar evidently has grown tired of Kumara, and plans to have Doris take her place. Kumara wouldn't stand for that, naturally, and it's certain that she's strongly opposed to what Amkeddar is doing, especially regarding the cult. That's two counts against her from Amkeddar's viewpoint." Corbin's tone took on a troubled note.

"Kumara quite probably saved our lives that night Amkeddar got the drop on us. He was going to do something pretty drastic, but she argued him out of it. I've partly paid her back for that by accidently ruining Amkeddar's plans for the night. He'll try again, though—and soon."

Melhorn said anxiously, "That means Doris is still in danger of being forced to commit murder."

Corbin nodded with grave emphasis. "I've got to stop it somehow and save Kumara at the same time. This last isn't just a side issue. She'd be immensely valuable to us as a witness against Amkeddar. If we could get her to the police, she'd be only too glad to tell everything she knows in revenge for what Amkeddar tried to do to her." Corbin straightened sharply, snapping his fingers. "Or the other way around—get the police to her! It could be done. We could easily manage to have the police search Amkeddar's estate on the charge that he's breaking the new anti-vivisection law. And if we were along, to steer the search to Kumara—"

"That's it, Jeff!" Melhorn cried excitedly. "It's…why, it's beautiful. Once arrested by the police, Amkeddar could be forced to free Doris from his control…"

"We'll get Lorrimer in on it," Corbin added. "He'll be valuable to us in that he knows the people in Sylvan Heights, and can obtain affidavits from those from whom Amkeddar purchased animals. Many, if not all, must be decent people, humane enough to overlook profits and add their suspicious to ours. We'll get started as soon as it's light. Nobody would be interested in our ideas at this hour."

They had reached the driveway of the house. Melhorn turned into it, pulling to a stop before the garage.

"What are you going to do now, Jeff?"

"Watch for Doris to return. There's little doubt that she will. Amkeddar would hardly risk a kidnapping charge at this point, even though Doris would testify in his favor. He has too much to hide at his place. You may as well go inside and get some sleep."

MELHORN shook his head. "I'll watch with you. I wouldn't be able to sleep unless I was sure Doris had gotten back."

Corbin led the way from the car, suddenly aware of aching muscles and innumerable bruises. He and Melhorn glided quietly into the shrubbery bordering the driveway, from where they could once more watch the house and garden. They settled down to wait. The moon was low in the sky, but still bright enough to make close observation possible.

They didn't have to wait long. Fifteen minutes passed and a tiger came padding across the moonlit lawn, approaching from the lower end of the driveway. It paused a moment near the bottom of the terrace steps. Corbin stared as he made a discovery. The tiger held something in its mouth—something that seemed flat, oblong in shape, and black.

Corbin glanced appraisingly at Melhorn. The other's face mirrored a startled question. Shrugging slightly, Corbin peered once more at the steps. The tiger was gone, apparently having ascended.

Corbin moved his eyes along the terrace, to the French windows of Doris' room. Presently an ethereal white shape rose from below the concealment of the balustrade, straightening as though from a stooping position. It was Doris. She gazed a moment at the garden, then turned. The French windows swung open and closed. Quiet fell.

Corbin waited for what he judged was a safe interval. Nothing else happened. The quiet remained undisturbed. Finally Corbin nodded at Melhorn and stood up.

"It's all over—for this time, anyway."

Melhorn said, "I'd certainly like to know what that object was that she carried."

"We can try to find out in the morning. For the time being, it would be best to leave her alone."

They entered the house from the front. In the upper hall, near the doors of their respective rooms, they paused momentarily.

Corbin said, "We'll have to be up as soon as it's light. There's a lot to do, and we can't give Amkeddar any time to prepare a defense—or offense."

Melhorn inclined his head. "I'll see that we're up in time, Jeff. Get all the sleep you can in the meanwhile. You need it," He gripped Corbin's arm in wordless affection, then turned into his room.

Entering his own room, Corbin began to undress, exhaustion weighting his movements. But when he had stretched out on the bed, sleep refused to come. He stared without seeing into the pale silver moonlight streaming through the windows nearby, thinking thoughts that were at once confident and despairing.

HE DIDN'T know how much later it was when a faint, almost inaudible sound reached him. He stiffened in sudden, complete alertness. Slowly, carefully, the door of his room was swinging open! He lay still after his first, involuntary motion, watching from beneath slitted eyes.

Ghost-like, a white figure slipped into the room. Doris! Corbin's mind flamed with wonder. What did it mean? The stealthiness of the girl's actions warned him that it could be nothing pleasant.

She closed the door softly, with almost no sound. Then she turned and began to creep toward the bed. In her right hand she held a small object that shone glassily. Her face had a somnambulistic lack of expression, which together with her deliberate, secretive advance was oddly frightening.

Nerves tense as a wound spring, Corbin waited and watched, hardly daring to breathe. Doris reached the bed, bent over it. A flash of sinister, dark purpose lit her tawny eyes. Now Corbin saw what it was that she held in her hand. Memory came to him with livid sharpness of the small black oblong that Doris earlier, in her tiger guise, had carried in her mouth. It had been a case, he realized now. A case for—

A hypodermic syringe, filled with a strange amber fluid.

Even as this final thought raced through his mind, Doris' hand descended in an abrupt, appallingly swift movement. The deadly needle shot like an arrow toward Corbin's arm.

CHAPTER ELEVEN
Council of War

CORBIN whipped aside with frantic speed. He felt the girl's fingers graze the skin of his biceps. At his motion, she recoiled instinctively, in shocked surprise, as though she had touched fire. Before she could recover, he whirled over on the bed and caught her wrist in a bear-trap grip.

Under the fierce pressure of his clutching fingers, she seemed to go wild. Oddly, there was nothing in it of fright, of terrified effort to escape capture. Rather it seemed the wildness of one thwarted in the fanatical pursuit of a mission, striving desperately to avoid failure.

She did not release the hypodermic.

She clung to it stubbornly, as though resolved to use it despite all Corbin's resistance. With all the strength of her lithe, athletic body, she heaved and twisted in a violent struggle to free her wrist. The nails of her free hand gouged into Corbin's flesh as she sought to pry his fingers loose. Her frenzied contortions made her hair swirl in tumultuous disarray over her face. Except for her labored breathing, she made no sound.

In his prone position on the bed, Corbin was at a disadvantage. Though stronger than the girl, he had nothing against which to brace himself for effective use of his superior muscles. Each time he tried to gather his legs under him, he was pulled once more flat on his chest. Doris had her bare legs planted firmly on the floor and was straining backward as she fought. To pull against her meant being drawn off the bed. He could only retain his hold on her wrist and suffer the torture of her clawing fingers. He could not let go for even the precious split-second it would take him to gain his feet. She was too furiously determined to complete the task for which she had come. He could take no slightest risk of the hypodermic being brought into contact with his body.

There was no poison in the hypodermic, he knew. Amkeddar would hardly adopt a course so dangerously obvious. What that needle most likely contained was a drug that would destroy his will, enslave him as Doris had been enslaved.

CORBIN was aware that Amkeddar had recognized him during the pursuit within the wall. There had been sufficient light streaming through the doors of the building where the interrupted ceremony had been taking place. Amkeddar had realized that Corbin had been spying upon the tiger ritual and had gained knowledge that in one way or another could be used against him. Corbin thus had quickly to be gotten out of the way. It had taken no great mental feat on Amkeddar's part to guess that Corbin was staying secretly at the Melhorn residence. And with Doris in the same house, a plan for preventing further interference from Corbin had been a simple matter. But Amkeddar had overlooked the fact that Corbin may not have been asleep when Doris searched for and found him.

Corbin, however, was grimly conscious that he was by no means out of danger yet. Slowly and inexorably, he was being pulled off the bed. He felt one of his legs touch the floor. It gave him a sudden idea. Working his foot under the bed to serve as a prop, he abruptly ceased pulling against Doris and lunged forward with his arm. It was unexpected. Straining backward, the lunge left her momentarily off balance. He gave her no opportunity to brace herself again. With his free leg now supplying the necessary leverage, he jerked her toward him.

The powerful tug had the effect of whirling her around. Her back hit the side of the bed. He held her pinned there, while he pulled himself forward on his elbows. His other arm encircled her, adding another grip to her wrist. Then, holding her with one hand and working with the other, he began to pry the hypodermic loose. It was anything but easy. In a fury of despair, the girl threshed and writhed, scratched and bit.

Persisting with bleak, dogged single-mindedness of purpose, Corbin finally tore the needle free, hurling it the length of the room behind him.

Only then did he release her. She scrambled erect, breathing heavily, her disheveled hair framing a face that was deathly pale and twisted with rage.

Corbin felt a sudden wrench of sadness. Gently, pleadingly, he grasped the girl's shoulders.

"Doris—snap out of it! You're not in your right mind. You'd never have allowed Amkeddar to put you up to anything like this if you were."

Furiously, she shook his hands loose. "Let go! Don't touch me! Haven't you manhandled me enough?"

"You're blaming me for this," Corbin said bitterly. "It isn't my fault. I had to protect myself."

"Why are you here—in this house? What do you think gives you any right to intrude in my affairs?"

"I'm trying to help you, Doris. Can't you understand that Amkeddar has some kind of devilish hold over you. He's making you do things—things like this—that you'd never consider doing if you were normal."

"That's a filthy lie! And what's more, I don't need or want your help. You're a snooping meddler." Her low, angry voice broke on a sob. "I...I hate you! I never want to see you again!" For an instant her tawny eyes fixed his with a glare of defiance. Then, whirling, she ran from the room.

CORBIN stood motionless, the girl's accusations burning like acid in his mind. A somnolent quiet followed her departure. The struggle, taking place almost noiselessly, had not aroused the other occupants of the house.

Finally Corbin stirred. He went to the door, swung it shut, and locked it. Switching on the light, he searched until he found the spot where the flung hypodermic had landed. It lay in scattered fragments on the rug. A damp splotch on the wall showed where it had hit.

One by one, he picked up the shards. He wrapped them in a spare handkerchief, which he deposited in a bureau drawer. Then he lit a cigarette, switched off the light, and went to stand before the windows. He was still there when the first gray light of dawn appeared in the sky.

Corbin was finishing breakfast, which had been brought to his room on a tray by the butler several minutes before, when Melhorn and Lorrimer entered.

After greetings had been exchanged, Melhorn explained, "I sent for George, here, the first thing I did this morning. Thought we'd give you a chance to dress and eat before dropping in." He peered narrowly at Corbin a moment. "What's the matter, Jeff, couldn't you sleep?"

Corbin grinned wanly. "Something like that."

Lorrimer said, "I hope I wasn't called out of bed so early just to prescribe a dose of sleeping tablets. What's this all about, anyway? Barton wouldn't reveal anything over the phone, except that you needed my help in a certain matter."

Corbin drained his coffee cup and lit a cigarette. Then he began swiftly to bring Lorrimer up to date on the events that had transpired since their last meeting.

He told of the failure of sedatives in keeping Doris in bed, to prevent her from paying another visit to Amkeddar. Next he told of his plan to follow Doris on another of her nocturnal trips, with the intention of forcing Amkeddar to release her from his control. He explained its outcome, describing all that had taken place, from the tigers that he and Melhorn had seen entering Amkeddar's estate, to the tiger ceremony and his near escape from death. He did not omit what he and Melhorn had witnessed upon their return to the house. Finally he detailed the facts and deductions reached thus far concerning Amkeddar's activities and the motives and people involved.

LORRIMER digested the information thoughtfully. A puzzled frown appeared on his blunt features. "You seem to have left something out—a possible explanation for the object which the tiger...Doris, that is...carried when returning here. There might have been a dangerous purpose for it, you know, considering the way you ruined Amkeddar's little party."

"There was," Corbin said. "I was saving that for the last." While Lorrimer and Melhorn watched on in perplexity, he rose and removed from the bureau drawer the handkerchief in which he had wrapped the hypodermic fragments. As he unfolded the handkerchief Corbin said, "The object Doris carried was a case—a case for this." He revealed the broken hypodermic.

Melhorn gasped. "But, Jeff, how in the world did you happen to get hold of it?"

"Doris brought it in last night, shortly after I went to bed. She had every intention of sticking the needle in my arm and injecting me with the fluid that was in the tube. I was lucky enough to be still awake, but as it was we had quite a little wrestling match before I got the hypodermic away from her. Too bad it broke. The fluid obviously was some kind of dope for making me highly susceptible to Amkeddar's charms. We could have used something like that against him."

Melhorn's face was pale with anger. "That devil! Using Doris for such rotten tricks. First the attempted murder of that Indian girl, and now this!"

"Any man capable of holding such evil power over the lives of innocent persons shouldn't be allowed to live," Lorrimer added. "With the malevolent intentions that

Amkeddar has shown himself to have, he's worse than a mad dog. And possessing a weapon in the form of a drug that destroys the will—there's no limit to what he may try." He looked grimly at Corbin. "After what you've told me, I'm more than willing to help you in any way I can. But what is there that I can possibly do?"

"First of all, I'd better explain my plan," Corbin answered. "The whole thing revolves around the Indian girl, Kumara. After the attempt on her life as a sacrifice in the tiger ceremony, she'll jump at the chance to get back at Amkeddar. The problem is to get her into the hands of the police. If it can be done, she'll spill everything she knows about Amkeddar, and he can be arrested and forced to free Doris from his control.

"WE COULDN'T bring Kumara to the police. That requires taking her right from under Amkeddar's hooknose, and after my excursion of last night, he's most likely just begging for me to pay him another visit. Only one thing is left to do—bring the police to Kumara. We can manage that quite simply by accusing Amkeddar of having broken the new anti-vivisection law and getting the police to search his estate. Once there, we can steer the search around to Kumara." Corbin nodded at Lorrimer.

"Where you come in is clear enough by now. Obviously, we can't just go to the police and get them to search on the strength of our suspicions. We'll have to have more or less definite proof. We'll need witnesses or affidavits from the people who sold Amkeddar animals, and from people who have heard animal screams coming from Amkeddar's estate. You know who these people are and where to find them. They trust you, and with you to act as our agent, there shouldn't be much difficulty in getting them to help us."

Lorrimer grinned confidently. "Don't worry about that angle. So many of them owe me unpaid bills that they'll be more than glad to do anything I ask. When do we start?"

"'At once," Corbin said. "The sooner the better, in fact. You can bet Amkeddar knows by now that his scheme to get rid of me has fallen through. He knows I'll strike at him again, and he won't be letting any grass grow under his feet."

"Let's go, then," Lorrimer said. "My car's outside."

CHAPTER TWELVE
Dr. Amkeddar Is Willing

CHIEF of Police Frank Rydell was a tall, gaunt raw-boned man who wore his dark blue business suit with the awkwardness of a backwoods farmer. He had pale brown hair that straggled over his forehead in lank wisps and pale blue eyes that were slightly watery and more than slightly apologetic. He gave the impression of one put into office on the basis of past favors received rather than ability, or perhaps simply because nobody else wanted the job. He looked tired and distressed, as though he worked hard all day to please everybody but found himself playing both ends against the middle.

Corbin, Melhorn, and Lorrimer had been in Rydell's office for almost an hour. Rydell had reluctantly and inexpertly questioned the four witnesses Lorrimer had managed to bring along. The witnesses had since been dismissed, and at present Rydell was engaged in reading through a sheaf of affidavits and bills of sale. He seemed to have difficulty keeping his mind on the task. When not shifting in his chair, he alternated between fingering his long nose and scratching, his bony jaw. His unhappy expression had increased.

Finally Rydell looked up. He cleared his throat hesitantly. "This stuff, here…it doesn't exactly prove Dr. Amkeddar has been doing what you said he was doing to animals. Vivisecting 'em."

"It's perfectly sufficient as a basis upon which to take action," Corbin said. He tried to keep out of his voice the growing irritation he felt. It had been a difficult and busy morning. Obtaining the witnesses and papers hadn't proved as easy as it had seemed in the beginning. And Rydell, with his timid skepticism and general incompetence, wasn't helping matters any.

"You're a lawyer," Rydell told Corbin. "You ought to know you got to have real proof if you want to charge somebody with something. I listened to what those people had to say, and I looked over this stuff, here, but I ain't seen or heard nothing yet to prove Dr. Amkeddar has actually been cutting up animals. Your case against him is just a lot of guesswork."

"I don't agree that it's guesswork, but considering it in that light, you'll have to admit it's mighty accurate," Corbin pointed out. "Why should Amkeddar buy cattle and sheep in the first place? To do his own butchering? Hardly likely. Even if he was willing to undergo all the unnecessary trouble and expense, the period of time between each date of purchase shows that he and his staff couldn't possibly consume the amount of meat involved.

"And there are the screams. When you butcher animals, you kill them as quickly and painlessly as possible. You don't torture them to death. Cows and sheep aren't in the habit of screaming. They do it only when in pain—which means when somebody's carving them up without first having bothered to kill them or render them unconscious. And that comes directly under the provisions of the anti-vivisection law."

"Lawyer's talk!" Rydell grunted. "You make it listen nice, but it still don't prove anything. You can't guess when a law is broke. You got to know. You got to have facts."

"Circumstances alter cases," Corbin persisted doggedly. "Sometimes it's necessary to carry out the spirit if not the letter of a law. This is one of those times. Indications if not facts show that Amkeddar is practicing vivisection. To allow him benefit of the doubt in the legal sense, may very well mean permitting him to continue indefinitely his torturing of helpless animals. And that violates every instinct of kindness and humanity written into the anti-vivisection law."

RYDELL scratched his jaw uncertainly. "I can't arrest Dr. Amkeddar just for maybe breaking a law."

"I didn't say anything about arresting him."

"Then what in tarnation do you want?"

"I want you to search Amkeddar's place to see if he has been practicing vivisection as indications show."

Rydell rubbed his nose and looked worried. "Dr. Amkeddar's a popular person hereabouts. Tied in with a lot of important people..."

Melhorn snapped, "If that's the only thing that carries any weight with you, then it might interest you to know that for every person who will support Amkeddar's side, I can obtain at least two who will support ours."

Rydell thought that over and began to look less worried. "But if we don't find anything, and Dr. Amkeddar sues or makes charges, it'd still be pretty tough."

"You can set your mind easy on that point," Melhorn said. "My friends and I will accept any and all responsibility for what may happen."

"All right," Rydell said. "I'll have a couple of the boys go out to Dr. Amkeddar's place this afternoon and look around."

Corbin put his hands on Rydell's desk. "Let's understand each other. The search is going to start right now, and we're going along. And you're going to be there to take charge of things. This may develop into something big. If it does, your men wouldn't be able to handle it alone."

"Say, what makes you think you can order me around?" Rydell demanded indignantly.

"I'll answer that," Lorrimer said. "We're just taxpayers. It's just our money that's paying you to do your job. And by heaven, if you don't stop this beating around the bush and do what it is plainly your duty, we'll see that you're replaced by someone who'll do it."

Rydell looked at his desk as if it were the only friend he had left. Then, shrugging bitterly, he rose. "I'll get things ready," he muttered.

SOME twenty minutes later, Lorrimer pulled his battered coupe to a stop before the gate in the wall enclosing Amkeddar's estate. Corbin was first from the car. He glanced back at the sedan in which Rydell and four detectives had followed. With reluctant slowness, Rydell climbed out. His men, however, appeared with alacrity, obviously eager for action.

One of Amkeddar's turbaned Indian servants was on duty at the gate. He wasn't Chondhas, Corbin noted. The Indian's black eyes surveyed the group expressionlessly.

"What do the *Sahibs* wish?"

"We want to see Dr. Amkeddar," Rydell answered.

"Who shall I tell the master is calling?"

"The police."

If any alarm appeared on the Indian's features, it was hidden as he performed a quick bow. "If you will please wait, I will inform the master." He turned and trotted swiftly up the driveway.

Watching, Corbin saw the man turn into the smaller building, where the tiger ceremony had taken place. He wondered tensely what Amkeddar's reaction would be. Would Amkeddar refuse to admit Rydell?

Within a few minutes, the Indian returned. He said nothing, but began at once to unlock the gate.

Corbin glanced at Melhorn in sudden anxiety. Melhorn's eyes were narrowed. He whispered, "I don't like this at all, Jeff. It's too easy."

Rydell and his four detectives had climbed back into their sedan. Following suit, Corbin, Melhorn, and Lorrimer squeezed once more into the coupe. They drove through the gate, stopping near the upper end of the driveway.

Amkeddar stood in the open doorway of the smaller building. He was dressed in a white laboratory smock and turban, and was drying his hands on a towel. As the two groups began emerging from the cars, he handed the towel to an Indian assistant behind him, also attired in a white smock and turban, and sauntered up casually. He surveyed the arrivals with a politely quizzical expression. His black eyes glittered icily when they settled on Corbin and Melhorn, but in another moment he concealed his reaction to their presence behind a smile of pretended delight.

"Ah, Mr. Corbin and Mr. Melhorn! So nice of you to visit me again."

Corbin grunted, "Your hospitality being what it is, we just couldn't stay away."

"Indeed?" Amkeddar's smile hardened at the edges. "I am honored—especially since you were considerate enough to bring representatives of the police to share it with you."

Rydell shifted uncomfortably. "This ain't exactly a visit, Dr. Amkeddar."

THE Indian looked surprised and pained. "Not a visit? Then will you be so kind as to tell me to what I owe the pleasure of your call?"

"We came to search your place," Rydell said.

"How interesting... And what do intend to search for?"

"These gentlemen, here..." Rydell indicated Corbin, Melhorn, and Lorrimer. "...have the idea that you've broken the new anti-vivisection law. They say you've been cutting up live animals in your experiments."

Amkeddar's surprise this time was genuine. And there was not a little bewilderment mingled with it. Evidently he hadn't expected an attack from this direction.

"I—practicing vivisection?" He chuckled in amusement. "I can assure you that is a lot of nonsense. My work involves experimentation with the glands of living animals. Vivisection is not connected with it, however. My method is based simply upon chemical injections into the bloodstream and their effects upon various glands as manifested by changes in temperature, pulse, respiration, and metabolic rate."

Rydell nodded understandingly. "Then you won't mind if we just sort of look around a bit?"

"Of course not! You are perfectly welcome." Amkeddar gestured—at the smaller building, from which he had emerged. "That is my laboratory. If you will kindly step inside, you will see that the charges against me are quite groundless."

Corbin decided that Amkeddar was being much too amenable. He felt a growing dismay as he followed the others into the building.

The laboratory proved to be just that—a laboratory. The tapestry, the throne-like chairs, the sacrificial block—all the ceremonial trappings, in short—were gone. Corbin's despairing gaze passed over neat, white worktables laden with apparatus, glass cabinets filled with bottles of chemicals, and a variety of animals in cages. Peering at the cages, he saw that they contained monkeys, dogs, guinea pigs, and rabbits. Three of the cages, especially large and set apart from the others, held tigers. One seemed to be asleep. The other two lay sprawled out at full length, regarding the intruders solemnly.

Corbin's thoughts were bitter. His position with Rydell would have been greatly strengthened had he been able to catch Amkeddar with the evidences of last night's ritual and massacre left intact. But the wily Indian all too apparently had anticipated that Corbin might bring the police. He and his four servants must have labored like demons to transform the building. Undoubtedly, the litter of blood and dead left by the tigers in their berserk attack upon the cattle and sheep outside, had also been cleaned up. Everything, in fact, which would have appeared even slightly suspicious, had most probably been removed.

CORBIN fought down his unease. Amkeddar had shown shrewd foresight in his precautions, but he couldn't have prepared for every eventuality. There was an excellent chance that Amkeddar had overlooked the possibility of Corbin striking at him through Kumara. The Indian girl, likely imprisoned somewhere in the house, was Corbin's ace in the hole.

Amkeddar waved a lean brown hand about the room. "As you can see," he told Rydell, "my laboratory contains no equipment for practicing vivisection. You have my sympathy for having been brought on a fool's quest." His black eyes rested for an instant on Corbin. Mockery and triumph glittered in their depths.

Rydell nodded emphatic agreement. "Didn't think you was the type anyway, Dr. Amkeddar. Sorry to have bothered you." He glanced accusingly at Corbin, Melhorn, and

Lorrimer. "Well, if you gentlemen are satisfied, we might as well go. We've wasted enough of Dr. Amkeddar's time."

"Not so, fast," Corbin snapped. "I said Amkeddar was practicing vivisection, and I can still prove it."

"What do you mean?" Rydell demanded irritably.

Amkeddar chuckled, though his jet orbs had narrowed in sudden wariness. "Mr. Corbin, if I may be pardoned for saying so, is a little...out of his mind. Perhaps now he will insist that I have...ah...hidden the vivisection tools."

Corbin said evenly, "That's just what you've done." He looked grimly at Rydell. "I said I can prove it, and I will. Listen. Amkeddar has an Indian girl on his staff by the name of Kumara. She knows he has been practicing...vivisection. She's strongly opposed to it. In fact, she got in touch with me and asked me to bring the police because she was afraid to do it herself. Amkeddar got wind of what we were up to and hid everything. He's keeping Kumara a prisoner right now, since he knows she'll testify against him." Corbin swung on Amkeddar. "All right—where are you hiding her? If you're as innocent as you claim, bring her out so that we can talk to her."

Amkeddar smiled slightly and shrugged. "I regret to say that Kumara has left my service."

"That's a lie!" Corbin shot out. "She's somewhere on this estate—and you know it!"

Amkeddar's tone hardened. "Very well, Mr. Corbin, if you're so certain of that, I invite you to search."

"I intended to do that anyway," Corbin grunted. He turned to Rydell. "Come on, let's get started. We'll go over the house first."

Features twisted in distress, Rydell shifted irresolutely. "But if Dr. Amkeddar says the girl left—"

"What he says means nothing to me," Corbin stated flatly. "Now are you going to come along, or do you want to hold hands with him while I search alone?"

RYDELL stirred reluctantly into motion. With an apologetic look at Amkeddar, he detailed one of the detectives to remain at the laboratory with the assistant. Amkeddar himself was to accompany them. Those arrangements made, he donned a martyred expression and started for the house.

The building was a two-storied, old-fashioned stone structure. Inside, it had been modernized and its numerous rooms fitted out with luxurious and exotic Oriental furnishings.

Rydell searched perfunctorily. The three detectives, however, were enthusiastic. Instructed by Corbin, they took special pains to hunt for concealed rooms and secret openings. But though the house was investigated thoroughly from top to bottom, no trace of Kumara was found.

Raging despair filled Corbin. He allowed nothing of it to show in his face. He wished to add no further satisfaction to the triumph evident in Amkeddar's thin-lipped, jeering smile.

As they strode from the building, Rydell told Corbin, "Hope you're convinced by now that the girl left like Dr. Amkeddar said. You could've took his word for it and saved us all a lot of trouble."

"I'm not through yet," Corbin growled. "There's still the laboratory."

Rydell opened his mouth, then closed it as he took in the expression on Corbin's face. He shook his head sadly, hopelessly.

Flanked by Melhorn and Lorrimer and followed by the three detectives whose enthusiasm was now definitely on the wane, Corbin strode into the smaller building. The detective left on guard there sat on a laboratory table, swinging his legs. The Indian assistant was perched on a stool, his brown face wearing a look of stolid patience. All three of the tigers were asleep now. The other animals stirred nervously, but remained silent.

Glancing about the laboratory, Corbin noticed a door at the far end. It gave into a large, littered storeroom. Assisted by Melhorn, Lorrimer, and the detectives, he proceeded to go through it. He found the ceremonial fixtures, each article having cleverly been scattered in various parts of the room. He shrugged. Placed away like this, out of their original setting, they meant nothing. He continued the search until at last it was painfully clear that Kumara was not present.

He returned to the laboratory. Ignoring the sardonic amusement on Amkeddar's hawkish face, he led the way outside in an examination of the grounds. This last resort proved as fruitless as the other efforts had been. Wearily, dejectedly, he strode back to the laboratory.

RYDELL stood in the doorway with Amkeddar.

As Corbin and the others approached, he faced them and demanded, "Well? Satisfied now?"

Corbin shook his head slowly. "Amkeddar is hiding the girl somewhere. He just seems to have been clever enough to have her taken a safe distance away."

Rydell emitted a grunt of disgust and turned to the suavely smiling Indian at his side. "Sorry to have put you through all this trouble, Dr. Amkeddar. But you understand that it ain't my fault."

"Of course," Amkeddar affirmed sympathetically. "Even those with the best intentions can be led astray by fools."

Highly gratified, Rydell shook Amkeddar's hand warmly and herded his detectives into the sedan. Melhorn and Lorrimer started toward their own car. Corbin lingered deliberately behind as a nebulous idea coalesced suddenly into grim purpose. Facing Amkeddar, he spoke softly, surely, and swiftly.

"This is the last time I'll try to be cute. From now on I pull no punches. So in fair warning I'll inform you that I'm watching Doris' windows at night in the garden. If she leaves again to keep a date at one of your filthy tiger get-togethers, I'm going to kill you. Do you understand? If she leaves again, I'm going to get you—one, way or another."

The Indian's face was cooly demoniac with the rage and hate he no longer tried to conceal. "So it's to be a shooting war, Mr. Corbin?"

Corbin nodded with bleak emphasis. "A shooting war Dr. Amkeddar." He met the furiously glittering black eyes before him in a challenge more eloquent than words. Then he spun on his heel and entered the car in which Melhorn and Lorrimer waited.

CHAPTER THIRTEEN
Trap for a Tiger

TRAILING clouds of cigarette smoke, Corbin savagely paced the floor of Melhorn's library. Melhorn and Lorrimer were seated in chairs nearby, gazing listlessly at the rug. Afternoon sunlight, streaming in a golden flood through the tall windows of the room, glistened on numerous bottles and empty glasses, indicating a mid-day repast that had been stimulating if not exactly nourishing.

"He had Kumara driven away somewhere—that's the only possible answer," Corbin announced at last, coming to an abrupt halt. "I happen to know Amkeddar has four male Indian servants. We saw only two at the estate. The other two must have been the ones who took her away."

"Maybe we should have hid out for a while and watched the gate," Lorrimer said. "If Amkeddar actually had the girl taken away, he'd have given an all-clear signal after our departure, and the two servants would have brought her back."

Melhorn shook his head somberly.

"Amkeddar's too smooth to have been taken in with a trick like that. Those preparations he made for our visit show that he thought of everything."

Corbin resumed his restless pacing.

"Those three tigers..." he mused. "I was too intent on the search to think of it at the time, but now the question arises of whether those three tigers were animal—or human. If human—" He stopped as though a wall had risen suddenly before him. "Three tigers! And Kumara and the two missing Indians—three!"

Melhorn sat up sharply in his chair, breath leaving him in a gasp.

Lorrimer said softly, "Good Lord..."

Corbin released a short, bitter laugh and dropped onto a couch across from the others. "That's the answer, of course. And it was under my nose all the time. What a blind fool I've been."

"Why blame yourself?" Melhorn said. "George and I didn't think of it either. And for that matter, if one of us had thought of it at the time, what good would it have done? Rydell was sick of the whole business, and if we'd told him our suspicions, he'd have arrested us all as a bunch of lunatics."

"Added to that," Lorrimer put in, "Amkeddar had Rydell eating out of his hand. He'd have denied our accusations, and Rydell would have accepted it as Bible proof."

MELHORN frowned puzzledly. "But if those three tigers actually were Kumara and the two missing Indian servants, what could have been Amkeddar's purpose in adding the two servants to the trick?"

"Simple psychology," Corbin said. "You see three where you're looking for one. Therefore it doesn't occur to you that the one you're looking for may be one of the three in plain sight. The purloined letter idea, with variations. And it worked—as we now know all too well."

There was a long silence.

Lorrimer muttered, "Looks like Amkeddar has us beaten at every turn. There doesn't seem to be anything that we can do now."

Corbin straightened suddenly, lips twisting in a hard grin. "I wouldn't say so. There's going to be a lot of action—and soon." He told Lorrimer and Melhorn of the parting exchange of hostilities between Amkeddar and himself.

Melhorn exclaimed, "But good heavens, Jeff, you told him you were watching in the garden. For all you know, he may come as a tiger—creep up on you!"

"Exactly," Corbin said. "I did it as a deliberate suggestion. If he shows up, I'll be waiting for him with a hunting rifle. And I'm pretty sure he'll show up. He may not see my warning as a trap, since I tried to give the impression that I was too angry with disappointment over the failure of our search to fully realize what I was saying. It seems to have gone over. Amkeddar wants me out of the way, as his attempt with Doris and the hypodermic last night shows. I know too much for his comfort, and in addition I've made myself too much of a nuisance. And after the search, he's most probably determined enough to get rid of me, to try doing it himself."

"You'll be taking an awful chance," Lorrimer pointed out. "Look—why not set a fancier trap? One in which there's greater certainty that it'll be Amkeddar and not yourself who's caught?"

"How do you mean—layout bear traps?"

"Something of the sort. A pitfall, for example."

Melhorn leaned forward eagerly. "I know just the thing...a spring-net! With a trap like that, you have your victim physically unhurt and easy to manage. It can be rigged up with little difficulty. And the whole thing can be arranged so that the victim can approach only in one direction—directly into the snare." He launched into a further, more detailed explanation.

Corbin and Lorrimer were enthusiastic. Swift plans were made for obtaining the necessary tools and equipment and carrying out the required work. Nora Melhorn was to help by taking Doris from the house on some pretext that would keep her away for the remainder of the day. No risk could be taken that Doris, seeing what was going on in the garden, might try to warn Amkeddar.

The blueprints of their scheme satisfactorily completed, the three men moved quickly into action.

MOONLIGHT bathed the garden like an infinitely fine luminous mist. Crickets trilled intermittently. A thin breeze made the surrounding shrubbery vocal with fretful rustlings and scratchings.

Corbin shifted restlessly on the damp grass. Uneasy thoughts kept recurring in his mind. Had he been wrong about the effect of his challenge on Amkeddar? Would the cunning Indian realize it as a trap, fail to show up? And if he did put in an appearance, would the trap work?

Corbin lay, facing the house, behind a large, semi-circular hedge situated on the side of the garden opposite the garage. The spot had been chosen carefully. It left Corbin in plain view of anyone approaching from the rear of the garden, the logical point from which an intruder would arrive who was aware that Corbin would, out of obvious necessity, be facing in the other direction, toward the house. And once sighted, the height and thickness of the hedge precluded an attack from any angle by the rear. A marauder with deadly intentions would thus be forced to walk directly into the snare arranged carefully a few yards behind Corbin.

This last consisted of a broad shallow pit covered with a net, over which lay a layer of leaves and soil had been spread. Thin cables led from the ends of the net to an anchorage near the top of a tall slender tree. More cables kept the upper half of the tree bent almost in a right angle. Anyone stepping into the net would set off a hair-trigger spring release, with the result that the tree would whip erect, the net engulfing the victim and, lifting him several feet into the air.

The unnatural position of the tree itself would not be noticed in the darkness, since other trees enclosed it on all sides, their thick foliage acting as a screen. The cables were practically invisible amid the dense shrubbery. Much exacting labor had gone into making certain that the arrangement would remain undetected until it had served its purpose.

Corbin and the others had realized early in their preparations that the net would hold a man, unaided by tools, indefinitely, but would not stand up long under the sharp talons of a tiger. Provision for this had been made in a novel way. Melhorn had rented a light, enclosed truck. If the trap were sprung, he intended to drive into the garden, directly up to the net, which, with its captive, would then be swung into the truck and released. Once its doors had been closed and locked the truck would serve excellently as a cage. The truck was concealed within the garage. Melhorn and Lorrimer sat inside it, waiting for their cue.

Knowledge that Melhorn and Lorrimer were close at hand added nothing to Corbin's peace of mind. If the trap failed, death would strike too swiftly for help to reach him in time.

CORBIN resisted the temptation to peer behind him. Even now the tiger might be crouching in the shadows at the rear of the garden, watching. The movement would warn that its arrival was expected, and consequently that a trap of some sort had been laid.

Tension mounted within Corbin as the taut, straining seconds passed. His ears were filled with the whisperings of shrubbery moving in the breeze. He listened intently, sifting the sounds. There—what was that? A tawny form moving a branch as it slid forward? Taloned forepaws trodding dried leaves?

Time and again the muscles of his back crawled in dread expectation. But no alien sound broke the murmuring quiet. No lithe, muscular form leaped crushingly upon him.

Paradoxically, he became filled with despair. Wouldn't Amkeddar ever show up? Had he been warned somehow that a trap had been laid?

Certainty that the whole idea was futile grew within Corbin. He considered the thought of giving up, going to bed. Bed...sleep... He was tired. It had been a busy day. Weariness ached in his muscles. Rest was what he needed—rest from all the worry and all the waiting.

The grass was soft. It gave under him alluringly. No mattress had ever been as deep and inviting. A delicious numbness spread over him like a warm blanket being tucked in around him by gentle hands.

Then—a low, eager growl, the thumping of paws on turf. And swift—so swift! Sleep drained from him like water from oiled cloth. Every sense thrilling in wild alarm, he whirled to see the striped demon bounding toward him, fangs bared, yellow eyes blazing in evil triumph.

A tiger! *The* tiger!

CHAPTER FOURTEEN
Backfire

AND then—a thwanging metallic sound, a hissing like a giant's sharply indrawn breath. The onrushing form disappeared as suddenly and completely as though the very air itself had swallowed it.

There was a high-pitched snarl of utter dismayed surprise. The next moment an object like a huge pear swung into Corbin's line of vision. It was alive. It writhed and twisted frantically, changing shape, now elongating, now drawing itself into an irregular sphere. It emitted sounds—grunts of rage and panic. And then it was gone as it swung, pendulum-like, back out of sight. The noises it made, however, continued.

With a yell of pure joy, Corbin leaped to his feet. "We've done it! We've got him! Quick, now! Quick!"

The garage doors squealed open. A car motor roared into life. Headlight beams knifed into the darkness blindingly. Gears clashed. The headlights swung toward Corbin, came rushing over the grass.

The next few minutes were chaotic with whirlwind action. To Corbin it was as vivid as repeated flashes of lightning across a night sky, but as disjointed in sequence as a nightmare. He knew only a screaming sense of urgency, mingled impossibly with a vast thundering delight. Dimly, as though the motions were being performed by someone other than himself, he was aware of running crazily to meet the truck, of shouting directions as it maneuvered into position near the insensate thing swinging helplessly in the net and now clawing at it savagely. Then Melhorn and Lorrimer were beside him, at once elated and grim with purpose.

"I'm going to lower the net," Melhorn said. "When it's down far enough, swing it into the truck."

"And hurry!" Lorrimer urged. "The net won't hold much longer."

Corbin found himself moving again, in that sharply defined but dream-like state. The huge pear swung suddenly before him, writhing, snarling. He heard Lorrimer speak.

"Careful! Don't get too close." There was the rattle of a block and tackle, a thin squeaking. The pear descended, gyrating furiously as it came.

"Watch out for those claws!" Lorrimer implored. "Wait for its back to turn toward us. Then shove... Now!"

Corbin was pushing, exerting his strength in feverish effort against something loathsomely warm and twisting madly under his hands.

"He's in! He's in! We've got him," Corbin cried.

"Throw in the lines and close the doors!" said Melhorn. "Quick—before he gets out of the net."

The cable, looping it, fumbling it, almost dropped it and having to start over. Then throwing it into the dark square mouth, hideously vocal. The slam of stout metal doors, the sharp clicking of a lock.

Over. Finished.

CORBIN leaned against the truck in abrupt limpness. They had done it. Full realization of the accomplishment struck into him stunningly.

Amkeddar was caught!

Back at the house, lights blazed suddenly. Within seconds, two figures appeared on the terrace. Descending to the lawn, they began to run toward the truck. Corbin saw they were

Nora Melhorn and the butler. The noises attending Amkeddar's capture had evidently aroused them.

Corbin glanced at the windows of Doris' room. Light glowed behind them. As he watched, they swung open and the slim figure of the girl appeared on the terrace, to stand, gazing curiously toward the group in the garden.

"For pity's sake, what is this all about?" Nora Melhorn demanded as she hurried up.

"Indeed, sir," the butler told Melhorn. "I thought a riot of some sort was in progress."

"Nothing to be alarmed about," Melhorn said. "We've merely been...uh...catching rats. Yes—catching rats."

"A likely explanation!" Nora Melhorn pursed her lips and donned the expression of a woman who senses that there are secrets from which she is being excluded. She gazed in narrow-eyed interest at the truck, but it was quiet now, revealing no clue to what was locked inside.

Melhorn patted her spare shoulder. "Everything is all right, Nora. We'll explain later. For the present we're going to be very busy. Now go back into the house. And don't worry."

"Stay with Doris," Corbin added with soft insistence. "Keep her in her room. Don't let her out of your sight for any reason."

Partial understanding of the situation dawned in Nora Melhorn's eyes. She nodded quickly and turned to hurry back to the house.

The butler said eagerly, "If I may be of service, sir..."

"We have everything under control, Wallace," Melhorn responded. "You can go back to bed."

"Yes, sir. Thank you, sir." Face clouding with disappointment, the butler started away.

Quiet fell. From within the truck came sounds of soft movement, stealthy, questing.

Corbin glanced at Doris' windows again. Silhouetted in their light, he saw Nora Melhorn leading the girl inside. Lips tightening purposefully, he turned to the truck.

"Amkeddar!" he called softly. "Can you hear me?"

"Quite well, Mr. Corbin," the muffled answer came.

"We've got you—you know that."

"But not for long, Mr. Corbin."

"Long enough to accomplish what we want."

"And what might that be?"

"To free Doris from your control. Restore her completely to complete normalcy and we'll let you go. Refuse, and we turn you over to the police."

A DERISIVE chuckle issued from within the truck. "You would hardly do that, Mr. Corbin. After that little search party fiasco of yours this afternoon, the police are definitely on my side of the fence. Turn me over to them, and I'll charge you with kidnapping. And if you kill me or keep me prisoner, Doris remains in my power." The chuckle sounded again. "You are in no position to bargain, Mr. Corbin. If we do anything at all, it will be on my terms."

Corbin snapped, "You're overlooking something, Amkeddar—Kumara!"

Abrupt, utter silence.

"So she's still alive," Corbin said triumphantly. "You still have her..."

"No—I've had her taken away. You'll never find her."

"Too late, Amkeddar. You gave yourself away. She's still at your estate—and you know it. All right—now we bargain on my terms. Free Doris, and we let you go. Refuse, and we'll go and fetch Kumara and take her to the police. Not Rydell, but higher authorities, far more intelligent and efficient. You know what that will mean. Kumara knows plenty about your activities, and after trying to murder her, she won't hesitate to tell everything. You've probably broken enough laws to get a life sentence—or worse."

Amkeddar's voice grated like a file on steel. "Don't do anything you'll be sorry for, Mr. Corbin…"

"You refuse?"

Silence.

Melhorn drew Corbin aside. Lorrimer joined them, holding a rifle, which he had obtained a short time previously from the driving compartment of the truck.

"He's forcing our hand, Jeff," Melhorn whispered.

Corbin nodded bleakly. "Everything hinges on Kumara. He has her under guard, but evidently isn't too sure that we couldn't get her away. He's simply giving himself the benefit of the doubt. He knows that taking Doris out of his power is our primary objective, and that if we do get Kumara we'll bring her here to force him before contacting the police. Once we do that, he'll give in."

"Which means," Melhorn said, "that you'll have to run the risk of taking Kumara from Amkeddar's guards."

Corbin shrugged. "Nothing else to do."

"Then I'm going along. You'll need help. George, here, will watch the truck."

Corbin hesitated a moment, finally agreed. "We start at once. Amkeddar's men may get worried about his failure to return and be on the alert for trouble." He started toward his roadster, parked in front of the house.

CORBIN and Melhorn crept through the shadowy, weed-grown field, converging upon the vine-covered wall ahead. They had left the roadster a safe distance down the road, to avoid having the sound of the motor alert the guards within the estate. Both gripped revolvers, which had been obtained earlier in the day.

Reaching the wall, Corbin made a stirrup of his hands, indicating in pantomime that Melhorn was to mount this way to the top. He wished to take no chance that Melhorn might slip in climbing the vines. When Melhorn had gained the crest of the wall, Corbin joined him, moving swiftly but carefully. He paused a moment, surveying the enclosure with intently narrowed eyes. Light streamed through the partially opened door of the laboratory building, but no sound or movement broke the stillness of the scene.

Finally Corbin slipped to the ground. He helped Melhorn down beside him, listened a moment, then started toward the gate.

One of Amkeddar's Indian servants was on guard there. He had slumped down against the wall at one side and was dozing—a fact which proved unfortunate for him. Taking due allowance for the turban which the man wore, Corbin clubbed him into further unconsciousness with the butt of his revolver. Then, gesturing to Melhorn, he turned toward the laboratory.

Peering cautiously through the opening in the door, Corbin saw that there were two persons inside. One was Kumara, huddled forlornly in a cage. The other was an Indian, whom Corbin recognized as Chondhas. Corbin smiled grimly. He had a score to settle with the man.

He thought swiftly. Chondhas held a rifle. He could cover the Indian before he could use it, but no chance could be taken that Chondhas might try to shout an alarm. Corbin had already had a sample of the Indian's tricks.

Corbin decided to use a trick of his own. Softly and indistinctly, he called, "Chondhas!"

The Indian started to his feet, gazing toward the door. He voiced a question in his own language, hesitating.

Corbin repeated his call, making it more demanding. Chondhas paused a moment longer, shrugged, and started for the door. Corbin moved to one side of the opening. As the Indian swung the door wider and stepped outside, Corbin hit him. He used his fist this time, aiming for the point of the Indian's jaw. Chondhas dropped as though he had been struck by a pile driver.

"That makes us even," Corbin muttered, rubbing his bruised knuckles. He gestured to Melhorn and strode into the laboratory.

Kumara stared in wide-eyed incredulity as they appeared. "You!" she gasped. "But how—?"

"How isn't important." Corbin said, examining the cage. "We're here."

"What do you want?" A dim hope struggled in the Indian girl's face.

CORBIN gave a quick nod of assurance. "We came to get you out of here. Where's the key to this lock?"

"It's in a drawer, there." Kumara pointed eagerly to a table near Corbin.

The key was one of a dozen or so, fastened to a ring. Several had to be tried before the one that opened the cage lock was discovered.

Aided by Corbin, Kumara climbed stiffly from the cage and stood erect. "Free!" she exulted. "Free! It seems too good to be true. I had given up hope long ago." Abruptly she gripped Corbin's arm. "But how were you able to reach me? Where is Amkeddar?"

Rapidly Corbin explained, revealing his capture of Amkeddar. He went on to tell of his efforts to release Doris from Amkeddar's control, describing the part Kumara could play in bringing about complete victory. He finished by saying, "I know you probably blame Doris for everything that happened, but you must realize by now that it isn't her fault. Amkeddar's the one who's responsible. In return for your own freedom, then, will you help us to win freedom for Doris?"

"Gladly," Kumara responded. "I'll even do more. I'll show you a way to do it yourself."

"You can!" Eagerness and disbelief mingled in Corbin's involuntary exclamation. "But how?"

"It is done by means of a potion, which, given to a subject, destroys the will. You have only to state the nature of the change in the subject's mind that you desire, and it is at once accomplished. Hypnotism isn't necessary. Amkeddar uses it only to obtain special effects. Thus if you wish to return your Doris to normal, you have only to administer the potion and command that it be done. The potion leaves the body soon after, restoring the will, but the change in mind remains. It is all fiendishly clever, as you can easily see. Given the potion and told that such and such a thing is so, a subject continues to believe it even after the return of his will, and does, in fact, use his will to fight all efforts to make him believe that it is not so."

"Just the thing," Corbin whispered delightedly. He caught Kumara's shoulders. "Do you know where I can find some of this potion?"

SHE nodded her glistening black head. "I do—but it is locked away. Obtaining it would take time. And time is precious. Amkeddar must be placed in the hands of the police as quickly as possible. The man is a devil. Don't be too sure that he will remain in your power indefinitely."

Reluctantly, Corbin agreed. "We'll leave at once, then."

"First I must find the amulet," Kumara said. "It can be used as a weapon against Amkeddar should anything go wrong."

Corbin was puzzled. "The amulet?"

"You noticed the large gold ring, bearing the head of a tiger, which Amkeddar wears?"

"Why—yes."

"That is the amulet. Amkeddar has injected himself so often with the elixir of change, that it is only through the power of the amulet that he can retain human form. When he adopts tiger form, the amulet naturally must be left behind."

Corbin nodded understandingly, but the information left him dazed. Unorthodox science, or black magic—which one was the true answer to Amkeddar's weird practices? Corbin wasn't certain. He knew only that, after the incredible events of the past several days, anything might be possible.

Kumara spoke again, her voice quickening. "The amulet most likely will be at the house, in Amkeddar's room. I will go alone. The two others of Amkeddar's men, off duty now, are asleep there. If I go alone, there will be less possibility of waking them."

"All right," Corbin agreed. "But hurry."

"I must have the keys you took from the drawer. They will enable me to enter any part of the house."

Corbin had unconsciously been holding the key-laden ring. Reminded of it, he turned it over to Kumara, and she hastened from the room.

Alone with Corbin, Melhorn released a deep sigh. "Almost over, Jeff. It's hard to believe. Soon the whole affair will seem just a bad dream."

"I hope so," Corbin said. "But I'm afraid there are things I'll never forget...things that will always haunt me."

They fell silent, waiting, while the leaden minutes crept past. Then, with a soft rustle of sound, Kumara stepped into the room. Her face was triumphant.

"I have it," she announced. "Come, now, let us go."

Wild elation surging through him, Corbin led Melhorn and the girl in an eager dash from the building. Down the gravel driveway, they raced, toward the gate.

CORBIN knew the gate was locked, but the guard he had slugged would have the key. Reaching the spot where he had left the guard, he received his first hint of what seemed to be impending disaster.

The man was gone.

There was an abrupt rustle of shrubbery from behind. In unison with Melhorn and Kumara, Corbin whirled around, all of his senses keening in dismay.

Covering them with a rifle, stood a naked apparition. It was Amkeddar, features twisted in a demoniac grin. Two figures accompanied him. One was the guard, restored to consciousness, holding a rifle also. The other was—Doris. She clutched a coat about her, evidently belonging to the guard. Corbin realized in a far corner of his mind that it must have been as tigers that Doris and Amkeddar had arrived on the scene.

"Drop your guns!" Amkeddar commanded Corbin and Melhorn. "Hesitate for just so much as an instant, and I shoot."

There was nothing else to do. To resist would be to commit useless suicide. Corbin released his grip on the revolver, heard it join Melhorn's in a fall to the ground.

Amkeddar walked toward Corbin slowly, eyes blazing, lips writhing back from his teeth. His voice was low, quivering with hate. "We settle accounts once and for all, Mr. Corbin. But first a little reward for your cleverness tonight." Without warning, he swung the barrel of the rifle against the side of Corbin's head.

Awareness left Corbin in a flash of intolerable brilliance.

CHAPTER FIFTEEN
Dr. Amkeddar Plays Host

DARKNESS, in him and around him, vast and complete. Then a vague sensation of shock. The darkness brightened. He became aware of pain, repeated, insistent. A dull anger surging through him, he opened his eyes.

The first person he saw was Amkeddar, garbed now in a white laboratory smock. Corbin realized that the other had been bending over him, apparently having been working to restore him to consciousness. Now, with a nod of satisfaction, the Indian straightened.

"Delighted to find you awake at last, Mr. Corbin. You were delaying festivities."

"I'll do more than that if—" Corbin abruptly broke off. In attempting to move his arms, he discovered they had been bound tightly behind his back. Other discoveries came. He was wet, drenched. Water, it seemed, had been poured over him to bring him awake. And his cheeks burned from numerous stinging slaps.

He was in the laboratory, he saw, lying against one wall. Near him stood Kumara and Melhorn, their faces drawn and pale. The arms of the pair had also been bound. Then he saw Doris at one end of the room. She wore a laboratory smock, too, her face indifferent and remote. Amkeddar's four Indian henchmen moved about amid noises of activity, engaged in tasks Corbin didn't try to identify at once.

The laboratory had undergone a change. It was this that explained the industry of the four Indians. The cages, tables, and cabinets had been placed around the walls, leaving the middle of the room bare. At present the Indians were occupied in setting up certain of the ceremonial fixtures Corbin had seen before. The throne-like chairs rose at one end of the cleared space. Around the edges were the braziers on their tripod supports. They were being lighted.

There was something definitely ominous about the proceedings. Corbin felt a coldness creep through him.

Amkeddar's voice sounded, amused and mocking. "I hope you find the preparations interesting, Mr. Corbin."

"You devil," Corbin gritted. "What are you up to?"

"You will see soon enough."

"How did you get out of the truck?"

"I summoned Doris to release me. The other woman had fallen asleep. Doris had no difficulty in leaving the house." Amkeddar chuckled gloatingly. "Leaving Doris so feebly guarded was a clumsy oversight on your part, Mr. Corbin. And very fortunate for me."

"But what about Lorrimer?" Corbin demanded in sudden anxiety. "What happened to him?"

"He is no longer alive, I am sorry to say. Doris struck him with a rock—a bit too enthusiastically. But it might comfort you to know that Lorrimer died without pain. He never knew what hit him. There was no warning, since I contacted Doris through my power over her mind."

LORRIMER dead! Doris his murderess! In an abrupt frenzy of rage and grief, Corbin threw himself against his bonds. But he had been tied carefully and securely. At last he gave up, panting. He felt blood trickle along his flesh where the skin had broken.

With a derisive laugh, Amkeddar turned away. He issued curt instructions to the four Indians, who had now finished their work. Two of them hauled Corbin roughly to his feet. The remaining two devoted their attentions to Melhorn, dragging him into the center of the room. Kumara was left unmolested. For some strange reason, she did not move from her position against the wall. Her features had a fixed, intent look.

Amkeddar busied himself for a moment at one of the tables. Then he returned to Corbin. In one lean dark hand he held a hypodermic syringe, filled with amber fluid.

Sight of the needle galvanized Corbin into another burst of furious effort. It availed him nothing. With his arms bound and an Indian gripping him at each side, he was helpless.

"Such exuberance," Amkeddar jeered. "I shall most certainly see that it has a more worthwhile outlet." He gestured insinuatingly with the hypodermic. "Perhaps you would be interested in my plan? Using the will-destroyer, I intend first to put you under my control—something that Doris unfortunately failed to do the other day. Then I will...ah...arrange to have you change form. In this form, you will be of great service to me by disposing of Mr. Melhorn."

"You must be completely insane," Corbin gasped. "You can't hope to get away with anything like that!"

"I do not hope, Mr. Corbin. I am positive that I will. After Mr. Melhorn has been taken care of, I will have the pleasure of dealing with you in an identical manner. My story to Rydell will be that you and Mr. Melhorn trespassed upon my estate and happened to be killed by one of the tigers that I keep for experimental purposes and which, through carelessness on the part of one of my servants, happened to escape from its cage. That tiger will be Kumara—slain in righteous indignation for her lack of manners toward my guests, even though they happened to be uninvited ones. As for Lorrimer, I intend later to return for him, load him into the truck, and drive it into a tree somewhere down the road. A regrettable accident, which will very nicely account for

Lorrimer's broken head. And when all is finally over, I will have Doris as a charming companion for as long as I shall be interested in her."

CORBIN sagged in despair. The scheme was diabolically clever. With various minor details taken care of, which Amkeddar in his broad outline had not mentioned, Corbin had little doubt but that it would succeed. As he thought of the role he was shortly to be forced to play, his mind rebelled in utter horror.

Amkeddar snapped out an abrupt command. The two Indians holding Corbin tightened their grips, keeping him pinned helplessly between them. Stepping forward, Amkeddar sank the hypodermic needle into Corbin's arm and pressed the plunger down as far as it would go. The whole action was accomplished before Corbin could gather himself for an effort at resistance.

In another moment, Amkeddar stepped back, grinning in satisfaction. "The dose I have just given you, Mr. Corbin, is a dozen times stronger than that which I gave Doris at Mrs. Castleton's party last week. You will feel its effects soon. The will-destroyer can be given either orally or intravenously. The intravenous method works somewhat faster, however, and is the most convenient for use on unwilling subjects."

In Corbin's mind began the impulse that would send him into a last struggle of outrage and despair. But the action was never completed. A strange feeling of indifference swept suddenly over him, quenching his intention as water quenches fire. The plan remained, but he no longer possessed the determination to carry it out. His will had gone. With it went his awareness of ego, of self. His thoughts became impersonal, detached. Nothing that had once seemed desirable and important to him mattered any more.

Amkeddar had been watching hawkishly. Now, with an eager, sadistic smile, he spoke.

"How do you feel, Mr. Corbin?"

"I feel…different."

"You are prepared to carry out fully and completely my slightest wish?"

Corbin nodded like an automaton. "Your slightest wish."

"Fine…" Amkeddar moved back to the table where he had obtained the hypodermic syringe. He selected another, filled this time with a greenish-black, oil looking fluid. At his command, Corbin offered his arm obediently. The needle sank into a vein; the plunger was pressed home.

SLOWLY, but with gathering speed, a sensation of dizziness rushed over Corbin. His blood roared deafeningly in his head. The room seemed to whirl crazily around him. He dropped to the floor, not all at once, but bending first to hands and knees. He had a vague, dim knowledge of pain. Giant hands seemed to be kneading his body, pulling and pressing at it as though it were clay.

Then the pain was gone, the dizziness was gone. The room steadied, came back into focus. Its outlines sharpened with crystal clarity.

Corbin stretched. He felt the muscles ripple along his new body. He was conscious of a boundless vitality, a savage, surging strength. Sounds came to him with a distinctness he had never known before. And he became aware of a host of fascinating odors and scents, which previously had never existed.

Leaving nothing to chance, Amkeddar pulled an automatic from one pocket of his smock and watched narrowly. Corbin shifted in growing restlessness, but made no move to attack. At last, with a nod of satisfaction, Amkeddar turned to Melhorn, still held in the center of the room. He said tauntingly, "Forgive me for having neglected you, Mr. Melhorn. My breach of manners, however, will soon be remedied."

Melhorn said nothing. He stared at Corbin, a sick horror naked in his eyes. His features were gray, sunken.

Amkeddar snapped out orders. Melhorn then was released, the ropes keeping his hands confined behind his back untied. Hopelessness showed in the sagging of Melhorn's shoulders as he glanced at the door. It had been closed and locked. There was to be no slightest opportunity of escape.

Again Amkeddar snapped orders. The four Indians moved in a group to one side of the room. Gesturing to Doris, Amkeddar seated himself in one of the throne-like chairs, the girl taking the other. Drums boomed suddenly. The wailing of flutes rose. A barbaric rhythm shaped itself, quickened in tempo. Throbbing, ululating, it swelled in volume, filling the room. Still it quickened, growing wild and intoxicating. And it began to call, at once pleading and demanding.

CORBIN heard the call. In a dim way, he remembered having heard it before. But now, with his will broken down, it was overpowering in its compelling insistence. He could no longer resist doing what it urged—to seek and kill, to slash and tear in a red orgy of madness.

His eyes settled on Melhorn. He felt a hot wave of eagerness, torturing in its intensity. His muscles quivered with impulses he could barely restrain.

The music, compelling, irresistible. Melhorn, warm and alive, flesh and blood.

He had to kill! *He had to kill!* He couldn't wait any longer. He couldn't control himself any longer.

He glanced pleadingly at Amkeddar. Stridently, gloatingly, the Indian laughed. He nodded. He pointed at Melhorn.

"Kill..."

With a growl of delight, Corbin padded toward his helpless victim, crouched to spring.

CHAPTER SIXTEEN
Battle of Tigers

OVER the throbbing of the drums and the wailing of the flutes came a shout.

"Stop!"

Startled silence dropped over the room like a muffling blanket. All eyes turned to the figure who had spoken.

It was Kumara. She stood near one of the flaming braziers at the edge of the cleared space. Her arms were free. Blood covered her wrists and hands like glistening red gloves, mute testimony of the supreme effort it had taken her to fight loose of her ropes.

She looked at Amkeddar and smiled. It was a quiet, somehow terrible smile. Then she reached into her dress. From some hiding place within it, she produced a small object that gleamed a dull yellow. She raised it high.

Amkeddar's face twisted abruptly into a mask of horror. He shot to his feet. He gasped incredulously and said, "The amulet... You...you have the amulet!"

Kumara's laughter trilled, cold and harsh. "Yes, oh lord and master, I have the amulet. It is only through the power of the amulet that you can now retain human shape. And that power is destroyed if the amulet touches fire! For your treachery and lack of faith, touch fire it shall..."

"No!" Amkeddar shrieked. "Don't—don't! I promise anything!"

Kumara's smile only grew more terrible. Amkeddar started toward her, then stopped, apparently realizing he could never reach her in time to prevent the amulet from being dropped into the blazing coals within the brazier. He spread his hands imploringly.

"Please, Kumara, anything… I promise you anything! I will release these people. I will give up my plans. You and I will leave here together, to take up our old life. Look, Kumara." Amkeddar reached into his smock, as though to produce something that would be incontrovertible evidence of his sincerity. In a blur of incredibly swift movement, he whipped out the automatic and fired, pressing the trigger repeatedly so that the roars of each shot seemed to blend as one.

But with a rapidity that almost but not quite matched Amkeddar's, Kumara had moved also. Only two of the bullets reached her. And before they did, she had dropped the golden tiger-head ring into the brazier.

INTENSE, vast silence followed Amkeddar's barrage. For an instant the occupants of the room stood frozen in motion, as though the air had turned to ice of incomparable clarity.

Then Kumara's hands went slowly to the front of her dress where now, below the heart, two crimson spots appeared and began to spread. She swayed. Her lips parted grimacingly for a laugh that issued instead as a sob.

Amkeddar stood rigidly, eyes closed, the lines of his face writhing in pain. A moment longer he stood thus. Then he dropped to hands and knees. The outlines of his body shimmered weirdly, flowed like molten glass. Colors blurred, ran together, changed. Presently came solidity, permanence. The transformation was over.

The tiger that was Amkeddar stepped from the limp, ripped folds of the laboratory smock.

Since Kumara's shouted order to stop, Corbin had not moved from his crouching position on the floor. There had been no counter-order. And no longer possessing any volition of his own, he could do nothing until commanded to do it.

Now he heard a growl. With detached interest, he saw Amkeddar tensing for a leap at Kumara.

Desperately summoning what remained of her ebbing strength, the Indian girl released a cry.

"Corbin! Amkeddar is your enemy. Fight him! Kill him!"

The will-destroyer had not yet left Corbin's system. He was still pliable, open to suggestion.

At Kumara's exhortation, purpose flowed into him. He had been given directions. He would obey.

Fight Amkeddar! Kill Amkeddar!

He flexed his powerful tiger's muscles. He snarled a challenge.

Amkeddar had frozen in dismay. Corbin as a source of danger had been overlooked. Reminded of Corbin now, warned of immediately impending attack, Amkeddar whirled to the defensive. Thwarted fury, a consuming, insensate hatred, flamed into his eyes.

Across a space of several yards, the two measured each other, fangs bared, muscles gathered with straining tautness. Then, almost in unison, they sprang to join in battle. They met to the floor. They wrestled for an advantage, rolling over and over, tawny bodies threshing and heaving. Each sought for a death grip on the throat of his adversary, while fighting savagely to protect himself from a corresponding attack. Back and forth, the battle raged, indescribably swift and violent.

Once they broke free. They circled each other for a moment, taking stock of damage inflicted, watching for any slightest relaxing of guard. Then, again, they crashed together in conflict.

Back and forth...rolling over and over...threshing and writhing biting and clawing...

AS THE battle progressed, Amkeddar's efforts grew more rational, planned, and deliberate. It was a duel from which only one would emerge alive. Amkeddar seemed to have realized that continuing it in blind, unreasoning fury was nothing more or less than suicidal. He began to fight with the stealthy cunning typical of him.

In a crafty maneuver, he allowed Corbin to swarm atop him, pinning his back to the floor. Then, with the claws of one hind leg, he struck at Corbin in a fierce effort at disembowelment. At the crucial instant, however, Corbin accidently slipped. The slashing claws merely grazed his flank.

Again Amkeddar got Corbin into a position where he could bring his deadly trick into play. But the repetition warned Corbin. Frantically, he rolled away—not a split-second too soon, for the other's razor-sharp talons painfully raked his side.

Now cautiousness settled over Corbin. Realization came that it was cleverness as much as swiftness and strength that would win. He fought carefully, refusing to be taken in by Amkeddar's deceptions.

The struggle resolved itself into a dueling match, in which the weapons were scythe-like claws backed by powerful tendons and driven by lightning-fast reflexes. The two combatants circled each other, darting in, dodging back, feinting, parrying, thrusting with blurred rapidity.

Occasionally they grappled, but each time they quickly broke apart. Neither wished to risk being drawn into a trap.

Feint, thrust, parry...feint, thrust, parry...around and around...

And then Corbin became aware of a growing weariness He could no longer move as quickly as before. He found that it was becoming strangely difficult for him to breathe. His lungs began laboring.

Amkeddar sensed that his opponent was weakening. He renewed his assaults with increasing vigor.

Corbin gave ground. A mistiness was growing before his eyes. Blood began pounding in his head. He felt a mounting dizziness that seemed oddly familiar.

With shock of horror, he realized suddenly what was wrong. Amkeddar had given him just enough of the elixir of change to accomplish, in tiger form, the murder of Melhorn. The time limit involved had more than been covered by the length of the battle. Corbin was changing back into human shape!

The realization dawned upon Amkeddar also. With a snarl of eagerness and anticipated triumph, he abandoned further caution and closed in for the kill.

DESPERATION brought a cold, nerveless clarity to Corbin. Only a trick would win now, he knew. If it failed, he was doomed.

Gathering his last reserves of strength, Corbin turned and ran. Amkeddar bounded in pursuit, eyes flaming with hungry malevolence.

A wall brought Corbin up short. He cowered against it, head drooping, panting laboriously. He seemed too weak to move. All fight, all spirit, seemed to have left him.

Gauging the distance between them, Amkeddar leaped in for the finish. Corbin darted aside at the last moment.

Amkeddar hit the wall hard. It stunned him for the precious instant Corbin needed. Before Amkeddar could recover and put up a defense, Corbin pounced upon him. Throwing his fast dwindling supply of strength into one final, titanic effort, Corbin closed his terrible tiger's jaws on Amkeddar's throat—ripped...tore.

Again.

And again.

Finally Corbin released the limp, blood-covered bundle of fur that had been Amkeddar. He slumped to the floor. A roaring filled his ears. The room gyrated madly before his eyes. The world rocked and spun beneath him. Then there was only a vast blackness. Exhaustion and the after-effects of the drugs with which he had been injected, had taken their toll.

And as he lay in stupor, Corbin began to change.

Chondhas had been waiting for that. He gripped his rifle more tightly. His dark features were anxious. While the battle raged, he had not been able to tell which of the two tigers was which. He had been forced to wait for the outcome. Now, as Corbin's change reached its weird climax, dismay and then rage contorted Chondhas' face. His eyes flashed vindictively at the slayer of his chief. He threw the rifle to his shoulder, aimed it.

Chondhas' three companions watched impassively. Melhorn, who had joined Kumara in an attempt to tend her wounds, cried out in horror. He started forward. The fact that he would not be able to reach Chondhas in time to prevent him from killing Corbin was appallingly obvious.

The imperative pounding of knuckles against the door struck like thunder into the tense silence.

"Open up!" a voice outside shouted. "This is the police!"

SLOWLY Corbin became aware of sunlight beating against his closed eyes. He opened them. He stared puzzledly. The laboratory was gone. The room in which he found himself was entirely different. But curiously familiar. Realization finally came that he was in his room, in Melhorn's home.

He stiffened as a chilling thought struck him. He whipped his hands from beneath the covers of the bed on which he lay and peered at them in apprehension. He sighed in relief. Human hands. Not taloned paws.

A soft chuckle abruptly sounded. "Awake, eh?"

Startled, Corbin twisted around. Melhorn stood at the other side of the bed, lips stretched in a broad grin. Beside him was…

Corbin gasped incredulously. It was impossible! He must be dreaming!

"I'm alive…all right," Lorrimer reassured. He fingered his bandaged head. "It was a close call, though. Doris swings a mean rock."

"I never was so glad to see anybody in all my life!" Corbin exclaimed. "Amkeddar told me you were dead—that Doris had killed you."

"Can't say she didn't try," Lorrimer responded with a grimace. "Luckily, I've got a thick skull and enough hair for a cushion. I wasn't completely out the first time she hit me. After she released Amkeddar from the truck, she bopped me several more times on his directions. That must have convinced Amkeddar I was done for. Even so, I wasn't unconscious long. When I woke up, I went straight to the police. Not Rydell, but the state police. I knew Amkeddar would go after you first thing, to stop you from getting Kumara."

Melhorn put in, "George and the police reached Amkeddar's estate in the nick of time. You had passed out from the fight, Jeff, and were beginning to...change. One of Amkeddar's servants—the fellow called Chondhas—was just about to shoot you. The arrival of the police changed his mind. He and the others now are where they can no longer do any harm."

"I imagine you had a difficult time explaining things to the police," Corbin said.

"Not too difficult. I simply told the truth of all that happened. Kumara bore me out, and the four Indians talked plenty once they got started. Whether or not the police completely believed everything is doubtful, but they agreed the whole affair is one that should be hushed up. Amkeddar has officially been charged with Kumara's murder. His disappearance will be explained as that he's hiding from the law. Nothing will be said about anything else. As for the dead tiger, it's just an animal after all. And a dead animal doesn't concern the police."

Corbin said softly, "Then Kumara is...dead?"

MELHORN nodded gravely. "But she lived long enough to clear up several things. Amkeddar's cult was a revival of an ancient Indian secret society. Originally, this society practiced a fantastic sort of devil worship, in which the tiger was regarded as an incarnation of Satan. The whole idea was tied in with sorcery of the blackest kind. As a mark of special devotion, the society's members had the ability to assume the physical and mental attributes of their evil patron. It was accomplished by magical elixirs and potions, the formulas for which, as Kumara seemed strongly to hint, were given the members by none other than Satan himself.

"If so, Satan evidently had plenty of strings attached to his gift. Too frequent use of the change elixir made it impossible to retain human shape. One dose seems to have lasted for some time, and while it did, the member could change shape at will. But the doses had to be repeated—and that's where the catch came in. To get around the elixir's chief drawback, the members were given a magic amulet in the form of a ring, which imparted the power to retain human form indefinitely. If the amulet happened to touch fire, however, this power was lost. The basic idea is frightfully logical, considering that tigers fear fire above anything else, and that Satan and fire are practically synonymous. In this way, apparently, Satan had an effective means of keeping the members in line." Melhorn smiled in wry humor.

"Here I am, discussing the most incredible things as though they were as real and commonplace as penicillin or radar. Science would say that an elixir capable of altering human shape was impossible—just a lot of superstitious nonsense. More direct-minded persons would simply call the nearest booby hatch."

"We're convinced, anyway," Corbin pointed out. "And after what I went through, I'm ready and willing to believe anything. But how did Amkeddar happen to get hold of the change elixir and the other things?"

"According to Kumara," Melhorn went on, "Amkeddar obtained the amulet and the formulas for the various magical drugs from records dating back to the original cult, which had come into his possession through a legacy. Most likely they had been in his family for generations, having been handed down from some ancestor who was a member of the cult. Amkeddar realized the elixirs would bring power and profit if used in the right way. And he was ruthless and ambitious enough not to hesitate.

"He opened a cult in India, but was forced to abandon it when one of the members got out of hand and killed an important government official. An investigation followed that would have landed Amkeddar in prison. But he escaped to America, gaining entry by means of forged and stolen papers. He represented himself as an Indian scientist specializing in glandular research, who had arrived to study American techniques. It wasn't difficult at all. He'd actually had scientific training, it seems.

"Amkeddar settled in Sylvan Heights for obvious reasons. It was small and remote, inhabited by people wealthy enough to make just the right kind of converts. From what Kumara told me, however, Amkeddar's purpose wasn't money alone. It was power, too. The will-destroying potion gave him absolute control over the minds and lives of his disciples. Those in Sylvan Heights were to serve merely as stepping-stones to persons in control of the country's economic and political structure. Amkeddar thus intended to become a sort of Svengali, with America, and ultimately the world, playing Trilby. Impossible? But with the will-destroyer, who knows how far he might have gone, if he hadn't been stopped in time."

THERE was a silence. Finally Corbin said, "And Doris? How is she?"

"She's been asking about you," Melhorn answered with a grin. "Kumara told me where to find a supply of the will-destroying potion, and it proved completely satisfactory. Working together, George and I brought Doris back to normal. She doesn't remember anything that happened."

"Later, we'll restore the other people Amkeddar got his hooks into," Lorrimer put in. "There's enough of the potion to go around. After that, the formulas go into the nearest furnace. The world can do very well without them. As for the possibility that some persons might have taken the change elixir too often, there's no danger. Amkeddar wasn't operating in Sylvan Heights long enough, and as final proof, there's the fact that no other amulet but his was ever in evidence."

"We have a lot to thank Kumara for," Corbin said, his voice gentle in tribute.

Melhorn nodded solemnly. "She made everything possible. But she wouldn't have cared to live. She loved Amkeddar, you know. He was thoroughly rotten, but she didn't see it that way until the end. He'd insisted that the cult and his use of the formulas was only a means of making enough money to settle on. Harmless enough. The cultists were having a killing good time, and could afford the high price."

There was a knock at the door. A soft voice asked, "Is Jeff awake yet?"

"He certainly is," Melhorn called back. "Come and get him..."

Doris rushed into the room.

Melhorn nudged Lorrimer's arm. "We might as well go down to the library. I have a bottle of rye that's begging to be emptied. As for Jeff, it seems that he's already well plastered."

"But lipstick isn't intoxicating, Barton," Lorrimer pointed out as he fell in step toward the door.

Melhorn smiled pityingly. "Then you've never tried it, George."

THE END

STRANDED ON AN ILL-MANNERED PLANET

It's not often we would describe a science fiction short novel as being "delightful" but that's exactly the word to describe J. F. Bone's wonderful tale, "Founding Father." It's the story of two small, lizard-like alien creatures—both vastly intelligent—who are stranded on a distant planet far from home. Bone describes these two creatures, Eu and Vin, as being similar in many ways to human beings, yet far beyond them in terms of intelligence and emotional control. In order to help them procure the materials needed to repair their crippled spacecraft and leave the detestable planet known to its inhabitants as "Earth," Eu and Vin employ (through implanted brain-control devices) the aid of two reluctant humans, Donald and Edith. These two human slaves prove to be a handful for their alien captors, with their wild fits of unpredictable behavior, unstable emotions, and fits of anger. But soon Eu and Vin come to the startling realization they are far more like their human captives than they could have dared imagine. "Founding Father" is full of unique, poignant situations that will leave you laughing out loud and give you pause to think about the ups and down of human frailties.

CAST OF
CHARACTERS

EU

This little alien creature was the smart one, physically weaker than his female companion, but always in charge because of his "superior" male intelligence.

VIN

Eu may have been the brains of the operation, but there was no doubt that Vin was his physical superior—even if she did spend most of her time riding around on the back of a naked woman!

DONALD

This fiction writer was just camping in the woods with his wife one evening. The next thing he knew he was a slave to a small alien lizard and making a fortune writing best-selling novels.

EDITH

She was a pretty young thing with a promising career in the motion picture industry, but that career hit a snag when she became the "pet" of a midget female alien.

ALICE AND THE REST OF THE GIRLS

There were six of them all told. Six young ladies whooping it up at a Hollywood bash. But sometimes too much to drink can lead to consequences of a most "alien" nature.

FOUNDING FATHER

By
J. F. BONE

ARMCHAIR FICTION
PO Box 4369, Medford, Oregon 97504

CHAPTER ONE

"WE need data," I said as I manipulated the scanner and surveyed our little domain of rocks and vegetation. "The animate life we have collected so far is of a low order."

"There is nothing here with intelligence," Ven agreed, gesturing at the specimens in front of us. "Although they're obviously related to our race, they're quite incapable of constructing those artifacts we saw on our way down."

"Or of building electone communications or even airboats," I added.

"I expect that there is only one way to get what we want—and that's to go looking for it," Ven said as she smoothed her antennae with a primary digit. "I also expect," she added acidly, "that there might have been other places from which it wouldn't be so hard to start looking. Or did you *have* to set us down in this isolated spot?"

I glared at her and she flushed a delicate lavender. "Do you think I landed here because I *wanted* to?" I asked with some bitterness, inflating my cheek pouches to better express my disgust. "There were less than two yards of useful fuel left on the reels when I cut the drives. There isn't enough to take us across this valley. We came close to not making planetfall here at all."

"Oh," Ven said in a small voice, vocalizing as she always does when she is embarrassed. Like most females, she finds it difficult to project normally when she is under emotional stress. Afraid or angry she can blow a hole in subspace; but embarrassed, her projections are so faint that I have to strain my antennae to receive them.

Her aura turned a shamefaced nacreous lavender. I couldn't stay angry with her. She was lovely, and I was proud to be her mate. The Eugenics Council had made an unusually good match when they brought us together. The months we had spent aboard ship on our sabbatical had produced no serious personality conflicts. We fitted well, and I was more happy than any Thalassan had a right to be.

"We shall have to try other measures," I said. "Although there aren't very many natives hereabouts, we had better start looking for them rather than wait for them to look for us." I felt disappointed. I was certain that we made enough disturbance coming down for them to be here in droves, which was why I had the robots camouflage the ship to look like the surrounding rocks. There could be such a thing as too much attention.

"They could have mistaken us for a meteor," Ven said.

"Probably," I agreed. "But it would have saved a great deal of trouble if one of them had come to us." I sighed. "Oh well. It was only a hope, at best."

"I could explore," Ven offered.

"I was about to suggest that," I said. "After all, the atmosphere is breathable although somewhat rich in oxygen, and the gravity is not too severe. It would be best to wait until dark before starting out. There may be danger. After all, this is an alien world, and Authority knows what's out there."

Her antennae dropped, her aura dimmed to gray and her integument turned a greenish black. "It doesn't sound pleasant," she said.

THE sun dipped below the horizon with an indecently gaudy display of color. After the last shades of violet had faded, I opened the airlock and watched Ven, a darker blot in the darkness of the night, slip away into the shadows.

She went unarmed. I wanted her to take a blaster, but she refused, saying that she had never fired one, wouldn't know what to do with one, and that its weight would hold her back. I didn't like it. But I was unable to go with her, and it was better that she did as she wished at this time.

I sat for a while in the entrance port watching the slow wheel of the stars across the heavens, and for a moment I wished that I were a female with the rugged physique to withstand this gravity. As it was, the beauty of the night was lost on me. I breathed uncomfortably as the pressure crushed my body and made every joint and muscle ache. Males, I reflected gloomily, weren't what they were in the old days. Too much emphasis on mind, and not enough on body, had made us a sex of physical weaklings.

I wondered bitterly if a brain was as worthwhile as the Council insisted.

The next few hours were miserable. I worried about Ven, imagining a number of unpleasant things that might have happened to her. I dragged myself into the control room and fiddled with the scanners, trying the infra and ultra bands as well as the normal visible spectrum in the hopes of seeing something. And just as I was beginning to feel the twinges of genuine fear, I heard Ven.

Her projection was faint. "Help me, Eu! Help me!"

I stumbled to the entrance port, dragging a blaster with me. "Where are you?" I projected. I couldn't see her, but I could sense her presence.

"Here, Eu. Just below you. Help me. I can't make it any farther!"

Somehow I managed it. I don't know from where the strength came, but I was on the ground lifting her, pushing her onto the flat surface of the airlock—clambering up—dragging her in and closing the lock behind as. I looked down at her with pride. Who would have thought that I, a male, could lift a mature female into a ship's airlock even against normal gravity? I chuckled shakily. Strange things happen to a body when its owner is stressed and its suprarenals are stimulated.

She looked up at me. "Thank you," she said simply. But there was more behind the words than the bare bones of customary gratitude.

I HELPED her into the refresher and as she restored her tired body I pelted her with numerous questions.

"Did you succeed?" I asked.

"Better than I expected."

"Did you find a native?"

"Two of them." The cubicle glowed a pale green as her strength came back.

"Where?"

"Two vursts from here—down the hill. They're camped near a road. They have a big ground car with them."

"Did you see them?"

"Yes."

"What did they look like?"

The radiance in the cubicle flicked out. "They're horrible!" Ven said. "Monstrous! Four or five times our size! I never saw anything so hideous!"

"Did they see you?"

"No, I don't think so. They weren't looking in my direction at first. And I don't think they can mentally sense, because I was frightened and they didn't respond to my projection." She was beginning to recover.

"You couldn't have been too frightened," I said. "I didn't hear you—and you can reach farther than two vursts."

"Mostly I was repelled," Ven admitted.

"Why?"

"I don't know. They smelled bad, but it was more than that. There was something about them that made my antennae lie flat against my ears. Anyway—I did a foolish thing." The cubicle turned a pale embarrassed lavender.

"What did you do?" I demanded.

"I ran away," Ven said. "And I made a lot of noise."

"All right—all right," I said impatiently. "Go ahead and tell the rest of it."

"By the time I stopped running I was down at the bottom of the hill," Ven said. "I was dead tired—and with all that rock to climb to get back to the ship. I didn't really think I'd make it."

"But you did," I said proudly. "You're a real Thalassan—pure green."

The cubicle slowly brightened again.

"Can you find them again?" I asked.

"Of course. I wasn't lost at any time. If I hadn't panicked, I'd have been back a whole lot sooner."

"Can you go now?"

SHE shivered with distaste. "I can," she said, "but I don't want to."

"That's nonsense. We can't let a little physical revulsion stop us. After all, there are some pretty grim things to be seen in this universe."

"But nothing like this! I tell you, Eu, they're horrible! That's the only word that can describe them."

"Take a stat projector—" I began.

"Aren't you coming?" she asked.

"Two vursts on this planet? What do you think I am?"

Her face hardened. "I don't know," she said coldly, "but I do know this—if you don't come, I won't go."

I groaned. From her aura I could tell she meant every word. It angered me, too, because Thalassan females usually don't defy a male. "Remember," I said icily, "that you're not the only female on Thalassa."

"We're not on Thalassa," she said. Her aura was a curious leaden color, shot through with sullen red flares and blotches.

"I have no right to force you," she went on stubbornly, "but I *can't* handle them alone. You simply *have* to come."

"But Ven—I'm a physical cipher. This gravity flattens me. I won't make it."

"You will," she said. "I'll help you. But this job needs a male mind."

It was deliberate flattery, I suppose. But there was an element of truth in it. Ven obviously couldn't do it, and obviously she thought I could. I couldn't help feeling pride in her need for me. I liked the feeling. For, after all, we hadn't been mated so long that there was too great an amount of familiarity in our relationship. The Eugenics Council had taken care of that very effectively when we announced our plans for our sabbatical.

"All right—I'll go," I said.

With a quick light movement she touched my antennae with her primary digits. The shock ran through me clear to my pads. "You're good," she said—and the way she said it was an accolade.

CHAPTER TWO

"THIS way," Ven said, emitting a faint yellow aura that lighted the area around her. "Follow me." She staggered a little under the weight of the equipment she was carrying. I wished that we had enough power to energize an air sled— but we had none to spare. The robots had used up most of our scanty power metal reserves in camouflaging the ship and the adaptor had taken the rest. This was going to be a miserable trip. It was going to be painful, uncomfortable, and perhaps even dangerous.

It was.

We went across rocks, through sharp-twigged brush, across the saw-edged grass of the meadow below us, over more rocks, and downhill along a faint double trail that never seemed to end. I was nearly dead with weariness when Ven's aura flicked off and the dark closed in. My proprioceptors were screaming as I sank to the ground and panted the rich air of this world in and out of my aching chest.

"They're just ahead," Ven whispered. "Around that next group of rocks. Be careful."

We moved forward cautiously. "There was a fire," Ven whispered.

"There isn't now," I said. "I can't sense any heat." The night air blew a rank odor to my nostrils. My spines stiffened! I knew what Ven meant when she said that these natives repelled her. I had smelled that scent before—the scent of our ancestral enemies! So *these* were the natives, the dominant life on this planet! I gagged, my tongue thick in my throat.

"You see?" Ven asked.

I nodded. "It's pretty bad," I said.

"It reminds me of a zoo," Ven answered softly.

I nodded. It did and it was thoroughly unpleasant.

I strained my perception to its limits, pushing it through the gelid darkness, searching until I found the natives. "They're asleep," I said.

"What's that?"

"Suspension of consciousness. Something like estivation."

"Oh. Then we can approach safely?"

"If we are quiet," I replied. "Sleep is broken easily and consciousness returns quickly."

The trail deepened beyond the rocks—two rutted tracks about three yards apart. We moved forward cautiously, our senses keyed to their highest pitch. The night was oppressively still and every movement rasped loudly. My breath came fast and shallow. My heart pounded and my musk glands were actively secreting as I parted the opening to their cloth shelter, and sensed the dim forms within.

"Stat," I projected and Ven handed me the weapon. It was almost more than I could manage in my weakened condition, but I aimed it and fired a full intensity blast at the nearest lumpy figure. It jerked and flopped inside its coverings, and the second form sat up with horrid speed!

A ROAR of sound came from it as the air was filled with its fetid odor. In panic I triggered a blast at the menacing figure, and it, too, flopped and laid still.

I ran my tongue over the roof of my dry mouth and called to Ven. "They're quiet now. Come in and see what we've got."

"Ugh!" Ven snorted as she entered the tent at my heels. "It stinks!"

"They're not the sweetest life form in the universe," I said as I prodded the huge mound beside me, looking for reflexes that would indicate returning consciousness.

"What are they?" Ven asked.

"Mammals," I said.

"No wonder I thought of a zoo," Ven said. "But they're so big!"

"Not on all planets," I said.

"Obviously," Ven commented. "Well—what's next? Let's get this done. I'm suffocating!"

"Hand me the probe kit," I said.

I selected two of the longest probes and made my way up to the head of the nearest monster. I scanned its braincase until I found the area I wanted and inserted the probes, driving them through the heavy bone and into the brain beneath. I clipped on the short antennae and stepped back. "Turn the control to low," I said. "Place the clips on your antennae. Now think of rising." The bulk beside me stirred and Ven gave a squeak of terror. "It's all right," I assured her. "Turn the control back to zero. This one's secure."

I went to the second and treated it like the first, and felt a justifiable pride as it reacted. Not many men could implant neuro-probes correctly on the first attempt. "All right, Ven. You can go out now. Take the controls with you. I'll see what I can do to get these brutes out of their coverings."

The tent opening swayed as Ven passed through and I bent over the nearest form. The covering was a heavy sack closed with a slide fastener much like the ones we used. I pulled and it opened, sending a flood of rank scent into the fetid air. I coughed, my eyes smarting, and found the fastener of the other sack. Retching with nausea I staggered out of the tent.

Ven sprang forward, caught me as I was about to fall, and lowered me gently to the ground.

"What are we going to do?" Ven asked as I lay panting at her feet.

"We're going to get them out of there," I said, "and take them back to the ship. I didn't come all this way for nothing." I drew one of the controls toward me, fastened the clips to my antennae, advanced the gain, and thought into it. There was a stir of movement inside and a huge form came stumbling out. It stood there clad in loose cloth coverings, reeking with halogen. I looked up at the dark bulk and shivered.

"That smell!" Ven said.

"WE can help it a bit," I replied and turned to the control. With its massive forelimbs the brute ripped the cloth from its body as it moved downwind. I made it stand and took the other control.

"Let me do it," Ven said. "You can't handle both of them in your condition."

"All right," I said, "but be careful."

"I will. Now what do I do?"

"Advance the intensity knob and think what you want it to do."

There was a flurry of movement inside the tent, the thrashing of a huge body, and the second mammal burst through the opening and staggered clumsily to a stop.

"Reduce the intensity," I said. "You're projecting too strong a stimulus. Now uncover it and send it over with the other one to cool off. They're more bearable when they're cold. They exude the scent from their skin glands to compensate for temperature."

"I know," Ven said. "I studied biology." She did as I instructed and then dropped beside me. We relaxed, gathering our strength for the climb ahead. But I didn't recover rapidly. I could move, but the exertion made me dizzy. The excitement was over and reaction had set in. "I'll never make it," I said dully.

"I can help," Ven said, "a little."

"It won't be enough. You don't have the strength to carry me." I looked at the huge bodies of the mammals gleaming pallidly in the darkness, and suddenly I had an idea. The Slaads on Valga domesticated mammals. They were quadrupedal, true enough, but they were still mammals. Why couldn't I ride one of these as they did? Those great masses of muscle should carry me easily. "I think I have a solution," I said.

"What?"

"I'll have one of them carry me."

"You can't!"

"Why not? They're controlled. And they're the only way I'll be able to get back to the ship." I picked up the nearest controller. "Let's see what happens."

Ven squeaked as the monster lifted me in the air and set me across its neck. I crossed my pads and hung on. The ground seemed terribly far away.

"How is it up there?" Ven asked.

"A little unstable," I said, "but I'll manage. Shall we go?"

We moved up the trail to the rocky abutment and turned up the hill. The brute beneath me climbed strongly and easily.

"Wait a minute," Ven said as she turned the corner behind me, "you're going too fast."

"Why don't you ride?" I called down to her. "This one moves easily enough. It's much better than walking."

"I think I will," Ven replied.

"THIS is all right," Ven said as we moved side by side up the hill. "The fibrils on top of its head—"

"Hair," I corrected.

"The hair of this one is longer than yours. I can hold on nicely."

The big bodies of the natives moved smoothly and powerfully, their giant strides eating up the distance we had so painfully covered some time before. Presently we came out onto the lower edge of the meadow below our ship.

Ven looked at me, her aura glowing pink with excitement. "I'll race you to the ship," she cried, and dashed off with a burst of speed.

Somehow I couldn't resist the challenge in her voice. I advanced the control knob and thought strongly. The brute jumped as though it had been whipped and leaped into a plunging run. I clung desperately for a moment and then relaxed as I caught the rhythm of the driving strides. My heart pounded, but not with fear. I had never known such exhilaration! Machines were pale compared to it. The mammal could run like a frightened skent—and it was faster than Ven's!

I caught her halfway up the meadow, and pulled away, exulting in the powerful muscles moving underneath me. I charged up to the grove of trees that concealed our camouflaged ship, and brought the mammal to a halt. It was panting, trembling, drenched with stinking sweat, but I didn't mind. I was part of it. There was a certain amount of feedback in a bipolar control circuit and I could feel the heat of its body, the beat of the great heart, the rise and fall of the broad chest, the pulse of the blood vessels in the thick neck. It was magnificent! I laughed. I had never before felt the ecstasy of physical strength!

I turned and looked back, still tasting the pleasure of the great body connected to my mind.

Ven drew up beside me. "Hai Yee!" she exclaimed. "What a sensation!"

"You liked it?" I asked.

Illustration by Bob Ritter

"Liked it? *Liked* it? I loved it! Didn't you?"

"I think so," I said truthfully.

"I'm going across the meadow again," Ven said as she turned her mammal around.

"No," I said. "We have use for these two and we have no knowledge of how much they can stand. There's no sense damaging them." I frowned as I noticed the bloody scratches on the legs and body of her mammal.

Ven noted the direction of my gaze. "They're not as tough as I thought," she said with sudden contrition. "But they're not too badly damaged, are they?"

"No." I said.

I ordered the mammal to set me down. Dawn was breaking and I could see better what we had captured. They were a male and a female. On the whole, except for their mammalian ancestry, they conformed to dominant-race criteria, being erect, bipedal, predatory types with binocular vision. Their upper extremities were evolved into manipulative organs similar to our primary digits.

The most outstanding difference was the extreme sex dimorphism, which was obviously apparent in the brightening light. The physical differences were carried to such lengths that it was hard to believe that they were members of the same species.

THEY weren't exactly ugly, yet there was something disturbing about them. Perhaps it was the rank halogen odor of their skin glands that were still secreting despite the coolness of the air. Or perhaps it was merely that they were intelligent mammals. It was as though Authority had, in a moment of cosmic humor, drawn oversized caricatures of Thalassans and endowed them with life. I felt a subtle insult in their presence. I suppose it showed in my aura because Ven came quickly to my side.

"I told you they were disturbing," she said as we looked up at their monstrous forms towering over us.

"I'm glad they're not uncontrolled," I answered, shivering a little as I looked at them. "I suppose it's just species antipathy, but they make me uncomfortable."

"Mammals were exterminated on Thalassa long ago, weren't they?"

"Yes," I said. "They ate our eggs."

Ven walked forward and ran her primary digits over the female's legs. "They're quite well evolved," she said. "The skin hasn't a vestige of scales."

"Neither does yours except at the tip of your tail," I said tartly. "Don't get the idea that they're a primitive life form. Actually they are a *later* evolutionary type than we! If our ancestors had not developed intelligence enough to realize their peril we would be extinct—and something like them would rule Thalassa today."

Ven shivered. "How horrible! I don't like thinking about it."

"Don't," I advised.

"What are we going to do with them?" Ven asked.

"I was going to analyze them and construct a proxy, but they're far too big to duplicate with our limited resources. I suppose the only thing we can do is to insert control circuits and use them as they are."

"Won't that be painful?"

"Only psychically. Physically they shouldn't suffer a bit. The brain, you know, feels no pain. It merely interprets stimuli from elsewhere."

"In mammals too?"

I shrugged. "I suppose so. Besides, what difference does it make? Once we're through with them we can destroy them if they're too badly damaged."

"That seems unfair."

"It's not a question of fairness. It's survival. If they don't perform properly, we shall have to dispose of them or they'll be back here with a whole herd. Of course, if they operate under control, we'll turn them loose when we're through with them. I doubt that their technology is advanced enough to recognize a bio-circuit if they saw one. And if it is, they will have learned nothing new."

"But why can't we keep them, take them back to Thalassa? They'd make an unusual contribution to the Central Zoo."

"I'm afraid not," I said. "I doubt if they'd survive space. The only part of the ship large enough to hold them would be the cargo storage compartment, and that's not shielded. A hyperjump would kill them. You wouldn't want even them to die *that* way, would you?"

Her aura turned gray. "No, I suppose not."

"There isn't a chance," I said, seizing her thought before it was uttered. "It would take ten of our lifetimes to reach our nearest outpost on normal spacedrive. Forget it."

"But—"

"Come along," I said. "I'll need your help to modify these brutes."

ACTUALLY it wasn't a hard job. Their brains were well developed and nicely compartmentalized. With our probes and instruments it was a simple enough matter to implant the necessary organic extensions of our instruments.

"That should do it," I murmured as I disconnected the leads I had jury-rigged into the analyzer. "They're clean as a Fardel's tooth." I was tired, but I had the pleasant feeling of accomplishment that comes from working with organic matter. Possibly if I were not so interested in History, I'd have become a medic. I do have a certain talent along that line.

At any rate, we now had a pair of proxies. With only normal fortune they would be completely undetectable.

"Is it all done?" Ven asked as she looked over my shoulder.

"Yes," I said. "But leave the probes in place until we test them." I dragged my weary body once again into the control room and tried the headgear and circuits. They functioned absolutely perfectly.

"What do we do now?" Ven's projection came to me.

"Remove the probes and send them back to their camp. There's no sense in leaving them here."

"But Eu—"

"No," I said. "They are not toys. They're tools. They're to do a job for us. Now stop acting like a child. When they bring us metal you can play games with them—but not now. They're stressed, tired, and need rest. And they're going to get it."

"Yes, Eu." Her projection was submissive.

"But don't worry," I added kindly. "You can monitor them. I installed two extra circuits, one to the hypothalamus and the other to the tactile centers. You will be able to feel every sensation they experience. It will be just like having an extra body."

"Can I try it now?" she asked eagerly as she came into the control room.

"Go ahead," I said. "Put on a helmet and use the double control. Take them back to their camp and then neutralize the controller. As for me, I'm going to the refresher. I need it."

CHAPTER THREE

I awoke from partial estivation with Ven's projection vibrating my antennae. "Eu! Come quickly! They're awake!"

I groaned. What did she expect? But it might be interesting to see how they behaved. And if they panicked, someone should be there to assume control.

I checked the chronometer. I had rested for eight satts, which should be more than enough. I felt about as well as could be expected, so with only a few choice Low-Thalassic expletives to help me I managed to clamber out of the tank and stagger into the control room. Ven already had one of the helmets on. I picked up the other and flicked the switch to "on." It was the male's—and he was talking. The words were gibberish, but the thoughts behind them were easy to read.

I was part of an entity called Donald G. Carlton, a male mammal of the human species. He was a "writer" and was mated to the female, who was called Edith and who worked in "motion pictures." They lived in a place called Hollywood, in a family unit structure faintly similar to a children's creche. Certain customs on this world dictated that the female of the species take one name of her mate, which indicated that the sex was even more subservient than female Thalassans. The male's body ached, but not near so badly as I would have expected. And, as I expected, there was no sensitivity in the brain.

"Hey! Edith!" Donald said. "Get up!"

"Leave me alone, Don. I'm miserable," a lighter voice answered from the lumpy sack beside him. "I had the most awful dream."

"It must be the mountain air," he replied. "I did too."

"Whatever made me think this would be fun!" Edith said. "You and your meteor-hunting." The sack heaved and twisted and her head appeared at one end. "I feel like I've been worked over with a baseball bat. Oh! My legs!"

"You're not alone," he said. "I guess it's the hard ground and these strait-jackets they laughingly call sleeping bags."

"About that dream," Edith said. "It was horrible. There was this little green and yellow thing that looked like a cross between a lizard and a human being. It was sitting on my shoulders and I was naked—carrying it around, doing what it wanted me to do! I wanted to throw it off and stamp on it but I couldn't. I just ran and ran and all the time that little monster sat with its legs around my neck, hooting like an owl. Now, wasn't that something?"

Donald was very quiet. "You know," he said slowly, "essentially that was the same dream I had."

"But that can't possibly be! People don't have the same nightmares."

"We did."

"Then maybe—maybe it wasn't a nightmare…"

"Nonsense. We're here. We're all right. But I think perhaps we'd better get out of here—oh, Keerist! I'm one solid bruise." He twisted around until he found the fastenings and opened the bag. With a groan he stood up.

Edith looked at him, her eyes wide with sudden terror. "Don," she said in a brittle voice, didn't you wear pajamas when you went to bed last night?"

"Yes."

"Well, you're not wearing them now." An expression of horror crossed her face. "And neither am I," she added in a small voice.

I COULD feel the shock in Donald's brain as he looked down at himself. "That's not all I'm not wearing," he said dully. "I'm shaved!"

There was a brief flurry inside the other sleeping bag. "So am I!" Edith's voice was a whisper of fright. "That was no dream! I remember this. The lizard gave me something that I rubbed all over myself—and my hair came off. I didn't want to, but I couldn't help myself." Her hands went to her head and she sighed. "Well, that's all there. For a moment I thought—"

"My skin is different," Donald interrupted thoughtfully as he inspected himself. "It feels thicker. And I don't feel cold, although I'll bet it's nearly freezing outside."

"Don! Don't you understand? That dream was real!" Edith said.

"Of course it was—unless *this* is a dream. We could be having a nightmare about a nightmare…"

I looked at Ven. "Just what did you, do to them?" I asked.

She glowed guiltily. "I didn't know it would take their hair off," she said. "I was worried about their scratches, and the insects were biting them. So I made them rub on some of our skin conditioner."

I raised my digits toward the sky. "There is an Authority that looks over fools and Thalassan females," I said. "What made you so sure our conditioner would work on them? It might have been poisonous."

"I tried it on the male first," Ven said.

"Genius," I breathed with icy sarcasm, "sheer genius!"

"Well," she said, "it worked!" The eternal pragmatist had applied her sole criterion. "And what's more they looked and smelled lots better after they used it."

I shrugged, gave it up, and turned my attention back to the mammals.

Edith had emerged from her sack and was standing before the male.

"Do I look like a nightmare?" she demanded.

"No. More like a skinned rabbit—ouch! What did you do that for?" He rubbed his face where she struck him with her digits.

"There!" Edith said. "*Now* do you think it's a dream?"

"I never did," he replied mildly. "I've never dreamed in my life. I was just breaking it to you easy. It was real enough—even the blank spaces. I wonder—"

"You wonder what?"

"What their reason was for capturing us and then letting us go. It doesn't make sense. They wouldn't grab us just for fun. They're obviously intelligent, and probably thought we would be useful to them. But they turned us loose. So we couldn't be useful except maybe for amusement—but that doesn't jell. No. They've done something to us. They've let us go for a reason."

"STOP analyzing!" Edith said. "Why don't you just get scared, like I am?"

"I am," he said, "but I like to figure things out. If I know what frightens me, it doesn't bother me so much."

"Do that while we're on the way home. Get your clothes on and let's get out of here! Right away!"

"We have to pack."

"Oh, leave it! Let's get out while we can!"

"I don't think we're in any danger," he said.

"Well—I don't want to stay here a minute longer!"

"All right. We'll go. But we'll pack first. Look at it logically. They had us cold. We didn't escape. We were *let* go. So why, if they didn't want us then, should they want us now?"

"Unless they can get us any time they want us."

"You have a point there, but if that's the case, they can get us anyway. So let's pack."

"You can pack if you want to. I'm leaving!" Edith pulled the opening to the tent and slipped out.

"Edith!" Donald cried. "Wait!"

I touched Ven. "Stop her," I said.

Edith's voice came from outside. "Don!" she called in a tight voice. "Don! Help me! *I can't move!*"

"Try coming back here and see what happens," Donald said slowly.

Edith's head appeared in the entrance. "I'm back," she said in a small voice.

"I thought you would be. Now let's pack and perhaps they'll let us go. It's obvious that we can't run away."

"But why? *What's happened to us?*"

"If I told you, you'd think I'm crazy."

"Tell me anyway. It can't be any worse than this."

"I think," Donald said slowly as he began to roll up his sleeping bag, "that we were kidnapped by extraterrestrials."

"Martians?"

"Not necessarily," he said. "But if I remember my nightmare correctly, they aren't human—and they are obviously smart. So they aren't of Earth. We don't have intelligent reptiles here. And with their ability to control our actions, I'd say that they were from a considerably higher culture than ours. They've done things to us—but I don't think they did them just for fun. They want us to do something."

"What?"

"I don't know. Right now I'd guess they want us to pack our things. Let's do it and get out of here. This place smells like the reptile house in the zoo!"

I WAS amazed. The native's analysis was as logical as my own would have been under similar circumstances. There was nothing wrong with his mind or with his courage. That big braincase held a smoothly functioning mind and a cold courage I could almost envy. In a similar fix I wasn't sure that I could be so calm.

My respect for him mounted. If there were others like him on this world, his race could be a potential danger spot for the whole Galaxy. And, with the natural antipathy between our races, these creatures could be *trouble* if they ever reached space. I wondered for a moment if Authority had known this when It brought me here. There must be some design that I should land here when this race was still capable of being frustrated.

For the sake of civilization I would have to learn more about these mammals. Much more. But since the male had deduced so much, there was only one logical course of action. I adjusted the filters on my helmet to allow the passage of surface thoughts, twisted the dials on the controller until the meters balanced and projected gently.

"Donald—listen to me," I said.

He stiffened. "I thought you would be somewhere around," he said. "Who are you?"

"My name is Eu Kor, and I am a native of Thalassa."

"Where's that?"

"A good many spatial units from here—a good many of your light years," I amended. "I mean you no harm, but I need your cooperation. My spaceship is crippled. Our fuel has deteriorated. We need more and I want you to get it for us. We captured you because we need your help. Being a native you would not make a ripple in this society. And we would create whirlpools."

"What is this material you want?"

"A metal. Atomic number 50, a white metal used as an alloy component of primitive metallic cultures," I said. "It shouldn't be too hard to get." I didn't realize how hard it was to describe what I wanted. I wasn't getting through, and it bothered me. The culture barrier was almost as bad as though we couldn't contact mind to mind.

"I think you mean tin," he said. I grasped the concept and it seemed right.

"Bring me some and I will run tests," I said.

"And what do I get in return?"

I THOUGHT quickly. If he wanted to bargain perhaps we could reach an agreement. It's always better to have a cooperative proxy. They don't cause nearly the trouble in management. And I had other things to do than monitor natives. There was a great deal of repair work to be done on the ship before she would fly again. The subspace radio power bank had to be rebuilt and the circuits should be checked.

"I can give you knowledge that you wouldn't have for decades—maybe centuries," I said. "And I can adjust your bodies for a longer and happier life," I shot a glance at Ven still immersed in her helmet. "In fact, I have made a few adjustments already."

"So I noticed," Donald thought dryly. "Although whether they're an improvement or not I couldn't say. But did you have to go to all this trouble?"

"Think of us—and discount the fact that you carried us because our bodies are too weak for your heavy world." I said. "Did you like us?"

"No," he said. "You repelled me. I disliked you on sight, more than I can say."

"The emotion is mutual," I said. "Yet I can endure you. But with your glandular outlook you could only think of destroying us."

"That is true. But you treated us like animals."

"You are animals," I said logically.

"We are masters of this world. We recognize no higher authority. We are free people—not slaves. And unless we are treated as free agents you will get no cooperation from us."

"I can force you to do as I wish," I said.

"Prove it!"

I took over. And while Donald watched with helpless horror his hand picked up a knife and drew it across his arm. The keen edge split the tissues neatly and the blood flowed.

"Don! What are you doing?" Edith screamed and then stiffened as Ven took control.

"Observe," I said as I released control.

"Why, you—" Donald began—and then continued in a tone of wonder. "Why—the cut's closing! There's no more blood...it's gone!"

"It's just one of the improvements I mentioned," I said smugly. "You also had a patch of scar tissue on your left lung and infected kidneys. You do not have them now. Had you not met us you would have been dead within five of your years."

HE was shaken. I could feel it. "I do have Bright's disease," he said thoughtfully.

"You had it," I corrected.

"All right," he said suddenly. "I'll bargain with you. You've done me a good turn and it deserves a payment. I'll help you get your metal." He grinned ruefully. "I guess I couldn't do anything else."

"It makes it easier this way," I said. I smiled to myself. I was telling him the truth, but not all of it. Nor did I trust him. There was fear and hatred in his lower centers, and a formless feeling in his upper levels that he could outsmart any damn lizard that ever lived. He didn't realize that I could read his surface thoughts.

"Just remember," I said, "I can control you completely, if necessary, and pick your brain for data whether you wish it or not. And forget those ideas of informing your authorities about us. Except with your mate you cannot communicate to anyone about us. There's a basic block in your brain that will result in irreversible mental damage if you try."

This last was not quite the truth. But I hoped that by establishing fear I would prevent talk. "Now find us samples of the metal I want." I withdrew and went back to scanning.

"What was going on there?" Edith said. "You were talking to empty air. And why did you cut yourself?"

"It was one of our reptilian friends," Don said. "Like I thought, they're right inside with us—every way. He's a weird sort. Wants to trade health and knowledge for tin."

"Tin?"

"Yeah. At least I think it's tin. His description of the metal fits. They use it instead of rocket juice."

"But that knife—your arm?"

"Look. No cut—no blood. That's one of the things they did to us. We've got puncture-proof skin."

"Is that good?"

"It isn't bad. And I don't think I'll ever have to shave again. As I remember I put that stuff on my face. Anyway, we now have a couple of fairy godmothers who ride around in spaceships instead of pumpkin coaches."

"You're mixing your stories," Edith said. "Cinderella travelled in the pumpkin coach, not her fairy godmother. And besides, it's not funny. We're more like those poor souls in the Middle Ages who were possessed by devils—incubuses, I think they called them."

"It makes no difference what you call them," Donald said indifferently. "Whatever they are, we've got them and they're not going to leave until they're damn good and ready. Incidentally, yours is a female, so she's probably a succubus. Now don't start screaming. You'll probably be paralyzed if you do."

"I won't scream," Edith said dully. "I'm too numb to scream."

CHAPTER FOUR

WE had surprisingly little trouble with the two natives once they realized we could control them if we wished. Of the two, Edith was the worst. She refused to cooperate and had to be forced into the simplest actions.

"We're going to have trouble with that one," I observed as Ven looked at me with faint exasperation in her yellow eyes.

"Oh, I don't think so," she said. "Not really. This is a normal female reaction. It's a phase. Like the way I felt when the Eugenics Council selected me to be your mate."

"Did you feel like that?" I asked with surprise.

"Of course. I wanted to make my own choice."

"But you never told me."

"There was no need. I came around to the Council's view before I met you. And Edith will come around to mine. Don't worry. I know how to handle this."

And she did.

I helped a little by altering a few reflex arcs and basic attitudes, but Ven wouldn't allow me to modify the higher centers.

"There's no need to make her a mindless idiot," Ven said. "You didn't do that to Donald."

"Yes, but Donald controls his emotions. He doesn't like me any better than Edith likes you, but he doesn't work himself into an emotional homogenate every time I make a suggestion. We argue it out like rational intelligences. Often I can use his experience and viewpoint. And when I can't agree, he will cooperate rather than operate under control.

He's not like that bundle of glands and emotions you are trying to make into a useful proxy."

"Well, she *is* a problem," Ven admitted, "but if I had her here—"

"That can be arranged," I said. "I'll give you two weeks. And if that doesn't work you let me perform a prefrontal block."

"That isn't very long."

"That's all we can afford, I told her.

"All right. I can try. In a month I know I could do it."

Donald protested violently when I told him what we planned for Edith, but when I gave him the alternative, he reluctantly agreed.

He passed a story that Edith would be visiting friends, and brought her to the ship.

At once Ven went systematically to work to reduce the mammal to an acquiescent state that would permit control. Since sleep is unknown to our race but necessary for mammals, the task of breaking down the female's resistance was simplified by physical exhaustion. Ven also found that the mammal's sleeping time could be used to strengthen the new reflex channels built during her waking periods. The results were amazing, even to me, and I'm fairly well trained in neuromanipulation. Halfway through the second week the mammal's surrender was complete.

"ANOTHER day and she can go back," Ven said. "I can finish her training at long range. Now that I have the channels established, I don't think she'll be any further trouble."

I took the helmet and scanned Edith. "Hmm," I said. "Do you know what you've done? You've built yourself into an Authority image."

"I know," Ven said smugly. "She is essentially a dependent type. Her mate was her decision maker. That's why I had to get her alone. It wasn't too hard once I knew where to look. As a girl, her mother made the decisions for her. As a woman, Donald has done it. And when I faced her with situations where she had to decide and where the decisions were invariably wrong, she transferred the decision-making power to me."

I looked at her sharply. "I had no idea that you intended to make a pet out of her," I said. "Otherwise I wouldn't have permitted this."

"Well, it's too late now. And besides, it was the only way I could do it in the time you allotted. But don't worry. She'll be as good a tool as your precious Donald—maybe even a better one—because she'll do things to please me and not merely because they're expedient."

Ven had a point there. But it isn't a good policy to get emotionally involved with alien races. However, the deed was done, and as long as Ven was happy I didn't care. I only hoped that she wouldn't become too attached to the creature.

Donald was much more cooperative and much tougher. He had realized from the start that there was no profit in objecting to my demands. But, unlike Edith, he gave me no handle for leverage. He arranged his life to include the unpleasant fact of my existence, and that was that. Where Ven achieved a form of mastery, I never received anything more than acquiescence. There were levels in Donald I could not touch. At first it irked me, but then I realized that I was the greater gainer. For Donald was a constant challenge, a delight to the mind, an outward collaborator, and an inward enemy. Our relationship had all the elements of an armed truce. And I often thought that if I did not have the crushing advantage of control, our contest might have been more even.

Although in time Donald's hatred became modified to a grim sort of tolerance, and his repulsion into something that closely resembled admiration, he never lost the basic species antipathy that separated us. And in that regard our feelings were mutual. The ancient Thalassan proverb that familiarity breeds friendship simply didn't apply. We held a mutual respect for each other, and in a fashion we cooperated, but I never could pierce the armor of resentment that shielded him. I tried, but finally I gave up. There would never be friendship between us. We were too different—

And too alike.

IN the days that followed the first contact, I proceeded according to approved methods of investigating alien civilizations. At my request, Donald went to the local book repository and we went through a number of works on law, government, social structure, and finance. I felt that I should have some knowledge of this mammalian culture before attempting to refuel the ship. There was no sense in calling attention to myself any more than necessary. If I could obtain what I wanted and leave quietly, I would be perfectly happy. This world was of interest—but it was too disturbing to contemplate for an extended period of time.

"You were right, Eu Kor," Ven said to me as we scanned the pattern of the mammals' culture. "If you had picked any place less isolated than this, we might have been engulfed in that maelstrom."

I nodded. "It was more luck than design," I said, "but I am happy that we are no closer. This world is not for us. It is too strange, too alien with its uncontrolled emotionalism and frightening energy."

"It reminds me of a malignant neoplasm," Ven said, "growing uncontrolled, destroying the body from which it draws sustenance. Have you ever seen such a seething flux of people, such growth—such appalling waste and carelessness?"

I shook my head. "The only parallel that comes to mind is Sennor."

"But that's a dead world—killed by a suicidal race that achieved technology before it had attained culture."

"Which is precisely the situation we have here. Or have you observed their social inequities and history? Periodically these mammals erupt in merciless riots and slaughters over things that could be settled by reason. And oddly enough, these 'wars' as humans call them have the effect of stimulating technology. This is a race that apparently loves death and battle. A barbaric horde of cultural morons, with a civilized technology geared to mutual destruction."

"Frankly, I've been scanning through Edith. I've seen only the technical excellence of their entertainment industry, and the enormous waste that goes into the making of one of their productions."

"We must have a synthesis," I said, "and pool our observations."

Ven nodded.

"I'm not at all happy about this place," I continued. "It makes me uncomfortable."

"Could we modify it?" Ven asked.

I shook my head. "It would take an entire task force to do that. Reeducation of this culture would have to begin at birth after appropriate culling. We would have to start from the beginning. I fear that the council would never authorize such an action on behalf of mammals. We are altruistic...but not that altruistic."

"Then they will destroy themselves?"

"I fear so. This culture has a poor prognosis. But it is perhaps better so. Or would you like to see them roaming through the Galaxy?"

Ven shuddered. "Not as they are now. Not these fierce, combative stupid brutes. Individuals perhaps, but not the race. They would have to learn the rules of civilization first."

"Yet they show no sign of learning. If they can't even cooperate with their own species, how in Authority's name could they ever get along with the dissimilar races of this island universe?"

"They couldn't. We would have to quarantine them."

"So isn't it better to save the expense and let them quarantine themselves?"

"I suppose so." Ven's aura was a dull gray and mine matched the gloom of hers. It is hard to stand aloof and watch a race condemn itself to death.

WE fed our observations into the analyzer, together with all extraneous data we could lay our digits on via our proxies—not to prove our conclusions, but to determine the means by which we could obtain the power metal with the least possible repercussions in this society. We both realized it would be fatal to expose ourselves. The mammalian technology was sufficiently advanced for them to duplicate the essential portions of our ship, and chaos could result if they secured a road to the stars. Generations of effort would be required to confine them again to their homeworld.

Thinking in this manner caused me to take certain precautions with the drive mechanism that would ensure no trace of our craft remaining if I projected a certain impulse at a given strength. Ven, of course, was appalled at my action, although she realized its grim necessity.

And in the meantime we worked with our proxies. I attempting to establish some means of quietly obtaining the metal we needed, and Ven doing nothing so far as I could determine that would further our mission. At that, Edith was in no position to obtain metal, and Ven was too young and inexperienced in contact work to attempt a mission of such delicacy. Since Edith amused her, I was content to leave them both to their own devices while I worked with Donald to speed our departure.

"In this society," I said to Donald, "it seems that one can accomplish anything with this medium of exchange you call money."

"That's close to a fundamental truth," Donald replied.

"And you are not too well supplied with it?" I asked.

"Those four ingots I brought you last week put a vicious dent in our savings account."

"Isn't your trade as an author profitable?"

"Only in spurts. It's a feast-famine existence. But it's the only one I care to lead."

"But popular fiction makes money—and you can write."

"I wish you'd tell that to my agent. He seems to have other ideas."

"I have recently read some of your fiction," I said, "and have noticed that it has certain basics that could easily be applied to an analyzer. There is no reason why we could not cooperate and produce a work that would yield a great deal of money."

Donald laughed. "Now I've heard everything!" he said. "You mean to tell me you could write a book *humans* would buy?"

"No, you would write the book. I would merely furnish the idea, the research data, the plot, and the general story outline. In your popular fiction," I continued, "there are four basic elements and a plot that can be varied about twenty-five ways. There is small need for philosophy and little need for abstract thought. In fact, there is no need at all for anything but glandular excitation. All that is really necessary is plenty of action, enough understanding of the locale and events to avoid anachronism—and the basics."

"WHAT are these basics?" Donald said. "As a writer I'd like to know them."

"There are four," I ticked them off on my digits. "First, violation of the ethical or moral code of your race; second, adequate amounts of cohabitation between the characters; third, brutality; and fourth—murderous assault."

"Hmm. Sin, sex, sadism, and slaughter," Donald commented. "You know, you might have something there."

"I have prepared an outline and a synopsis of such a book," I said. "It is a historical novel. It should sell. Most historical novels do."

"You've done what?" Donald gasped. Then he laughed. "Of all the insufferable egoists I've ever seen!"

"Listen," I said, ordering him to silence while I outlined the opening chapter.

"I can't stop you," Donald said. "But why should this happen to me? Isn't it bad enough to be bossed around by you lizards without having to be forced to ghost-write your amateur literary efforts?"

"It is laid in the period of your history called the Renaissance," I continued, "and deals with a young man of a noble but impoverished house who rose to power by cleverness, amorality, and skill with the sword."

"I suppose the girl is the daughter of the local duke."

"No," I said, "she is the favorite wife of a Saracen corsair."

"Well, that's a switch," Donald said. "Tell me more."

So I did. I outlined the opening and told him the major points of the whole story...as the computer had synthesized it out of seven excellent novels of the period and a four-volume set of Renaissance history.

Donald was enthralled. "You're right," he said. "It will sell. It's lousy literature, but it's got appeal. With this story and my writing we can out-Spillane Mickey."

He was more enthusiastic than I had ever seen him appear before.

"Who is Spillane?" I asked.

Donald looked at me as though he thought I was crazy and shook his head. "I can get to work on it as soon as I get home," Donald said. "And if I keep at it, it'll be ready for mailing in a couple of weeks. I'll get it off to my agent and we'll see. I hate to admit it, but I think you're right about the yarn. It should sell like hotcakes."

"That is fine. It should provide us with the medium of exchange, which is necessary in this society."

"It's not necessary," Donald grinned. "It's essential."

CHAPTER FIVE

DONALD'S prediction was a good one. The book sold—and sold well. Despite the outright plagiarism of ideas and source material it was hailed as a new novel—one that stimulated thought with its realistic approach to the life of the times. And we prospered amazingly.

With the advance money, I had Donald buy the land on which the ship was resting, together with the valley and rim rock. Having thus secured our landing site I felt a bit more comfortable. The comfort was even greater when, at Donald's suggestion, a fence was placed around the property and electronic telltales were installed. The remainder of the royalties was used to purchase tin and supplies.

But despite our prosperity and the regular supply of tin that came to me as a result of my adventure in fiction, and the certainty that Ven and I would be leaving, Donald was not happy.

As a successful new author he had to travel to meetings in various cities. He had to speak at public gatherings. He had to meet with publishers eager to receive rights to his next book. And Edith did not go with him.

Ven was adamant on this point. "It's bad enough that she is working on this motion picture," she said, "but I'm not going to have her traveling all over the face of this planet. She's the only amusement I have since we must stay cooped up in this place. I'm not going to let her go."

Donald was upset about it. He was so angry that he came to visit me voluntarily, and the sight of Edith's little car parked under the trees below the ship infuriated him even

FOUNDING FATHER

more. It took the controller to make him keep his distance as he stood in front of the airlock and hated me.

"Damn you!" he swore. "You can't do this to me! Edith's my wife and I don't like this relationship between her and that—that *dinosaur!* It isn't healthy."

"It's really out of my hands," I said. "Edith is Ven's responsibility."

"It's not only that," he raged. "Ever since you lizards butted into our lives Edith looks at me like I was a stranger." His face twisted. "I'll admit she has her reasons. But that gives her no call to ask Ven's advice rather than mine. When I told her I wanted her to come with me, the first thing she said was that she'd ask Ven. She doesn't do one damn thing without that cold-blooded little monster's consent! She even asks advice on what clothes she should wear!" He laughed harshly. "The blind asking advice from the blind!"

I COULDN'T help chuckling. Ven, like all Thalassans, had never worn anything in her life except a utility belt. Clothing has never been a feature of our culture. Since it isn't necessary on Thalassa, it was never developed, and since our sex impulses are periodic it has never been useful to attract either males or females. "I can see your point," I said. "Ven's ideas along that line would be zero."

"Not quite," Donald said angrily. "She likes moccasins. Apparently they make feet look more like your pads."

"Well?"

"But that's it! Edith's idea of what a well-dressed housewife should wear is—*moccasins!* She damn near caused a riot the other day when our TV repairman called to fix the set. We'll be lucky if we're not forced to move because of that little incident!"

"I'll speak to Ven," I said. "And if that doesn't work, I'll insert a block against such a thing happening again. I don't

180

want special attention called to you. That sort of thing will stop right now."

"Thanks," Donald said. "But I should be the one to stop it."

"Face it," I replied, "you aren't. Not now. But you will be once we're gone."

"Which can't be too soon to suit me," he said. "I spend every spare moment collecting tin for you. Edie doesn't. She *wants* Ven to stay."

"They seem to be happy with each other. Edith comes up here regularly."

"I know," he said bitterly. "She's here more often than she's home. I can't see what fun she gets out of running around these hills stripped to the skin carrying your, mate on her shoulders."

"I wouldn't know," I said. "Certainly you never seem to enjoy performing that service for me."

"I don't even like the thought of it. I'm not an animal, after all."

"But you are," I said. "So am I. The only difference is that I am a superior animal and you, being inferior, conform to my wishes. It is a law of nature that the superior type will inevitably rule. The inferior either conforms or dies. And you have no desire to die."

He shook his head. "But I can still object," he said.

"At that?" I asked pointing across the meadow with a primary digit.

Edith was running, her long yellow hair floating free behind her. Ven, high on her shoulders in a seat the two of them had contrived, waved gaily at us as they came up. Edith was flushed and laughing. Her eyes sparkled and her smooth bronze body gleamed in the sunlight. She lowered Ven to the ground, slipped the harness off her smooth shoulders, and stood behind my mate, breathing deeply but not at all distressed.

"OH, Donald!" she said. "We had a wonderful climb—clear up to the top of the ridge! And coming down was almost like flying! I'll tell you all about it in a minute, right after I take a dip in the pool. Ven doesn't like it when I sweat." She turned and ran down to the little pool in the meadow.

"See what I mean," Donald gritted.

"She seems happy. She's not hurt. And Ven's little weight doesn't seem to bother her. What are you complaining about?"

Donald growled something unintelligible, turned on his heel, and walked away.

I let him go. There was no sense in making him angrier than he was. After a moment the snarl of his car's engine rose to a crescendo then faded away into the distance.

A few minutes later Edith came back to the ship. "Why did Don leave?" she asked.

"Perhaps he had something to do," Ven said.

She pouted. "He's always so busy nowadays," she said sulkily. "He isn't nice like he used to be. Do you think he's tired of me?"

"No, I don't think so. He just doesn't like you spending so much time up here," I said.

"But it's fun—and Ven likes it," she said. "I like it too. And since he isn't home much anymore, it's the only place where I can relax and be myself." She brushed the drops of water from her body and shook out her damp hair. "It's wonderful up here—so quiet and peaceful—and Ven's so nice."

My mate's aura glowed a pleased pink as I turned an embarrassed lavender. It was almost criminal, I thought, what Ven had done to the girl. Donald might be my servant, but I had never attempted to condition him into liking it. As much as possible we operated as equals, rather than in this sickening relationship that Ven had imposed upon Edith. To avoid showing my displeasure I went up to the control room, donned my helmet, and went into rapport with Donald.

"I'm sorry," I said. "I hadn't realized the true situation. The best thing for both of us is for Ven and me to leave as quickly as possible."

"How quick is that?" he shot back angrily.

"Four thousand pounds more," I said.

"Whew! That can of yours must *drink* tin."

"It takes a great deal to leave a planet," I said. "And hyperspace demands a great deal more. Once we develop an inertialess drive it will be easier. But we've only been working on it a thousand years. These things take time."

"I imagine. Well, are you going to do anything about Edith?"

"No," I said. "It would only make things worse. The relationship has gone too far. Ven has become an Authority-image."

"You could break it."

"But I won't. I'm fond of Ven."

"You're a damned little tyrant," Donald said. "You like to see a human squirm."

"BE thankful that I'm the worst tyrant you'll see," I answered sharply. "You could really learn about them if the Slaads knew you existed. They're more advanced than you. And, unlike us, they're warlike and predatory. They breed mammals for food. However, I'll put up a marker on your moon before I leave. They respect Thalassa and won't preempt our claims."

"You mean you're going to lay claim to Earth?"

"Only technically. We'll exercise it only if the Governing Council decides it will be to our advantage."

"What would you do if you took over?" Don asked curiously.

"Clean things up," I said. "Stop wars, stabilize the population, increase production and distribution, give you an effective central government and an understandable legal code, and eliminate the unfit. In three generations you'd be Class VI all over your planet."

"It sounds good. What's the catch?"

"The catch," I said, "is that you wouldn't like it. You mammals are erratic, emotional, and uncontrolled. You do not reason well, and you have no race discipline."

"What's that?"

"The capability of sacrificing units for the benefit of the whole. Eugenics control, culling the unfit."

"You're talking about human beings!" Donald exploded.

"And what makes a human being different from any other animal?" I asked. "Would you hesitate to dispose of an animal that was unfit to breed?"

He sighed. "No," he said. "But that's not the same."

"What's the difference? And realize, it's done for your betterment."

"Just a bunch of murderous little altruists," Donald sneered. "Out of the kindness of your cold-blooded little hearts—"

"That's the trouble with you lower orders," I interrupted. "You get emotional. Your observations have no basis in logic. Actually, the Galaxy wouldn't even quiver if the lot of you disappeared tomorrow. Yet you think the universe rotates about your heads."

"I didn't—"

"Don't interrupt," I snapped. "You—your race—your whole pitiful little civilization is ready mentally and almost ready technologically to commit suicide. If we came and saved you, you would owe us eternal gratitude, but I doubt if we'd get it."

"You wouldn't," Donald assured me. "There wouldn't be a human alive who wouldn't hate you."

"I realize that—and that is one of the reasons I should report your world unfavorably to the council. We could hardly take on an altruism mission like this unless we felt that our work would be appreciated. It would be better to let you kill yourselves."

"Altruism!"

"In a sense. At least your race would be the greater gainers. All we'd get would be your excess population."

"And what would you want them for—slaves?"

"Authority, no!" I said, shocked in spite of myself. "We'd merely process them for food."

He was silent after that.

DONALD was away again, at a publisher's meeting. Our new book, set in Restoration England, was going to be an even greater success than the first if the advance notices were any criterion. Edith was at a studio party celebrating the completion of the picture in which she was working. And Ven was bored.

For a while she sat in on Donald's conference in a city called New York, but that proved to be uninteresting. I was busy with a faulty fuel feed in the drive chamber. The sun was hot, and the day was promising to be extremely warm even though it was not yet noon. It was one of those days when nothing happens, and I was grateful for it. I had had enough of emotional tangles to last me for some time. It was almost soothing to work with the robots on insensate machinery rather than supervise a pair of highly charged mammals and a hardly less unstable mate.

The association with these entities hadn't done Ven a great deal of good. In fact, I could notice a deterioration of her character that bothered me. She no longer looked at me with respect. Indeed, her yellow eyes at times held a pitying amusement that I should be so weak as to argue with Donald. I didn't bother to point out that the three tons of power metal had virtually all been brought aboard through Donald's efforts, and that our conveniences, our defenses, our robots and our very lives were due to the working arrangements I had established.

The only useful thing Edith had done in the past month was to help me change the tube liners in the steering jets. Her size and strength had made the job easy—and it was normally a hard one, since the robots didn't have the flexibility or balance that Edith, with her dancer's body, possessed. The job had taken two days. It would have taken better than a week if I had to use robots.

The mammals, I thought, would be of distinct value as members of spaceport maintenance crews. Their combination of immense strength and high intelligence would be useful to our society. I made a note of it and added it to the data I was assembling for the Council. It was foolish, perhaps, but I couldn't help feeling an interest in these creatures.

I looked across the little valley that was our domain. It was an idyllic life we were leading. Unhurried—peaceful—the sort of life I thoroughly enjoyed. It would have been perfect if it wasn't for the insane and dangerous world on which it was being lived.

Of course it was too good to last. Idylls invariably are. The peace of ours was shattered abruptly when Ven came into the drive room and disturbed my work. Her aura blazed a rich violet.

"Eu," she said. "Come on up into the control room. Something's wrong!"

"What," I asked.

"It's Edith. I can't do a thing with her."

"You're not supposed to. She's working now."

"She is not! Her studio has finished the picture and they're having a party."

"That's nice. I hope you're letting her have a good time."

"I told her to. But I never imagined what they'd be doing!" Ven's voice was anguished.

"Well, what are they doing?"

"Ingesting ethanol to excess!"

"Ethanol!" I gasped. "Oh no!"

I hadn't realized that normal mammals consumed excess amounts of the stuff, although there were references to it in the literature. I thought that was merely literary exaggeration. After all, we had been here scarcely half a year and we hadn't really learned too much about the details of mammalian society. Donald's kidneys had forced him to lead a quiet life, and the passing of Edith from his control to Ven's had caused no remarkable alterations in her doings.

I should have paid more attention to their customs. But I had been too busy. I swore as I reached for my control helmet. I'd have to stop this before it became serious. Donald would be of no help to me. He was several thousand vursts away, and even under the best circumstances couldn't be expected back for a day.

I didn't bother to call him, but instead adjusted the controls to Edith's setting.

CHAPTER SIX

A horde of gaily-dressed mammals surrounded me, their faces and bodies oddly fuzzy and distorted. Edith's voice was equally fuzzy. There was something wrong with her centers. I tapped the helmet and checked the controller just in case it was on our end, but they were functioning perfectly. There was nothing wrong—merely the fact that ethanol was disturbing the biocircuits I had implanted in her brain. I swore a few choice expletives of Low Thalassan and tried to get through by increasing the power. It did no good.

"I c'n still feel that li'l lizard in m' head," Edith announced. "Gimme another drink. I wanna wash her out. Darn li'l lizard makes me do things I dowanna do. It wants me to quit, but I wanna get drunk."

"Take it easy," a fuzzy male face said. "You're loaded. Why does a nice chick like you hafta be loaded? Whyncha get outa here? I gotta nice place over in Santa Monica where—"

The face disappeared.

"Hey! Alice! Golly, I almos' din't reckanize you. Howya doin?"

"Better than you, Edith. You're drunk. And from the looks of you, you're going to be sick if you don't get some fresh air."

"Gotta go spit in the eye of my li'l lizard," Edith said. "Y'wanna come with me? I got Don's car. We c'n get out a here an' get some fresh air—an' I c'n tell that li'l lizard what I think of her."

"What are you talking about?"

"You wanna see my li'l lizard. She's got yella eyes, and a li'l tail, and she turns all kindsa colors, and she lives in a rock with a door in it, an she makes me do things I dowanna do. It ain't so bad though. Mosta the time I like it. Not alla time though. That's why I wanna spit in her eye. She c'n tell me all she wants—but she's gotta leave me'n Don alone. I love that guy." Edith started sobbing—why, I couldn't understand.

"She's maudlin," I said to Ven. "No one's going to believe a thing she is saying. But this should be a warning to us. We'll have to put in a block against drinking ethanol. I didn't realize how badly it can affect the biocircuits." I handed the helmet back to Ven. "You can watch this mess if you want to. I'm going to our quarters."

I slipped out of the control chair and walked across the room.

I was stronger now, more accustomed to the gravity, and it didn't bother me unless I had to stand for long periods of time. I turned in the doorway to look at Ven. She had the helmet on again and her aura was a crackling red. I shook my head. Edith was due for a bad time when the effects of that hydrocarbon wore off.

I had hardly fallen into light estivation when Ven's projection crashed through my antennae.

"Eu! Get up! Come here quickly!"

With a groan I came slowly back to full facility and ran to the control room. Ven's face was filled with panic.

"They're coming up here," she said. "A whole earful of them!"

"Who?"

"Edith's drunken friends! Somehow she's collected six of them and they're driving up here to spit in my eye!"

Despite myself, I laughed. Ven looked so outraged I couldn't help it.

"We can close the airlock," I said, "and they can't tell us from a rock."

"I won't! I'm going to teach that girl a lesson she won't forget in a hurry! I've listened to myself being insulted for two hours—and she's still going strong. When she gets up here I'll show her whose eye she'll spit in!"

VEN was raging. I'd never seen her so emotional before. Her aura swelled and ebbed in ruddy shades as her breath came and went in short gasps.

"And how do you propose to do that?" I asked.

"I'll stat her!" Ven raged. "I'll stat every one of them!"

I blinked. "I wouldn't do that," I said mildly. "What can we do with them? The two we have are bad enough. And if you stat them, we'll have to kill or condition them. We couldn't let them go home with a story like the one they'd tell."

"I don't care," Ven said. "You can do what you like about the rest of them, but that Edith is going to learn a lesson." She was being emotional and quite unwilling to listen to reason—and she was larger and stronger than I. Despite my protests, she jerked a stat projector from the rack and strode toward the open airlock.

"Thalassa!" she exclaimed. "They're coming through the gate! They'll be here in a minute."

I could hear the roar of a protesting engine groaning up the trail to the lower meadow as I hurried after Ven. As I reached the airlock, the gray body of Donald's station wagon poked its nose around the trees below our ship.

Ven stood rigidly in the airlock, waiting, her lips tight and her eyes narrow. She took a firmer grip on the stat as the car stopped and the giggling, half-sober humans tumbled out. I was in a quandary. I didn't want Ven to shoot, but I couldn't close the airlock with her inside it. So I stood, hesitating while the group of gaily-dressed mammals came toward us through the trees, their high voices loud in the stillness.

"Gotta find that li'l lizard an tell her to stop meddling with my life," Edith's voice came to my ears.

Ven stiffened beside me as the group broke out of the trees in front of the ship.

"Why, Edie, it's beautiful!" a voice said. "It's a fairy glen! No wonder you'd never tell us where you got that suntan! And that big rock—it's just like you said— And—uh!" The voice never finished as Ven pressed the trigger.

I looked down at the six crumpled mammalian bodies and the lone standing figure that looked stupidly up at us.

"Well," I said. "You've done it this time. Now are you satisfied?"

"No," Ven said. "Not half." Her voice was tight with anger. She looked down at Edith. "Come here!" she said.

"Dowanna," Edith replied uncertainly. "You've made Don leave me. I don't like you." But habit was stronger than alcohol and under the furious lash of Ven's voice she came unsteadily forward.

"Do you understand me, you little sarf!" Ven snapped icily. "I said *come here!*" She took the control box from her waist and viciously twisted the intensity dial to maximum. At this range its force was irresistible, even with alcohol-deadened synapses. Edith shuddered and moved toward us, her hands clumsily tearing at the fabric that covered her.

"I'm com in'! You don' hafta shout. I ain't deaf. I ain't done nothin'!" She sat down beside the airlock and struggled out of her clothing, ripping the thin fabric under the last of Ven's anger until she was completely naked. Then she stood up and reached her hands toward Ven.

"You're not going to try to ride her while she's in that condition?" I said.

"This is my affair," Ven replied grimly. "I'm going to get this settled."

I shrugged.

THERE was no sense reasoning with her while she was in that mood. And if she wanted to kill herself that was her concern. I watched her drop onto Edith's shoulders, wind one hand viciously into the mammal's long blonde hair, and guide the gross body into a shambling walk toward the meadow. Edith swayed dangerously, but somehow she managed to stay on her feet as they disappeared into the trees.

I walked over to the six bodies, gave each of them a light stat to make sure they would remain quiet, and sat down beside the nearest one to think.

Ven's anger had left me a sizeable problem. What on earth could I do with six human females? I needed them like I needed a broken digit. Time passed and the sun rose toward the zenith, and finally I came to a decision. Since we had them on our hands, we might as well make use of them. Killing would be too dangerous.

And presently Edith came through the trees, a sick, tired, sober Edith whose face was dirty and tear streaked, carrying a grim Ven whose aura smoldered a reddish brown.

"What did you do to her?" I asked.

"None of your business," Ven snapped. "She's all right now. Aren't you, Edith?"

"Yes, Ven—and I won't do it again. Honest I won't."

"You'd better not," Ven said grimly. "Now I suppose we have some work to do."

"You certainly have," I said. "If it wasn't for your temper we wouldn't have this mess on our hands. Now get moving! Have Edith carry these girls to the ship." I gestured at the prone bodies. "And you...get inside and bring out the control equipment and connect the leads to the computer." I was angry, too. Under the force of my superior will, the two females scurried to obey. "I'm disgusted with you, Ven," I said angrily. "Just because your pet went to a party, you don't have to act childish. Did you expect she'd behave like a Thalassan?"

"I trusted her," Ven said.

"It just goes to show that you can't trust an animal too far," I said. "Now get moving. Bring the probes first. We have a lot of work to do before evening."

IT was finished sooner than I expected. The sun was still in the sky, but close to the edge of the hills. The row of mammalian bodies slumbered peacefully beside the airlock. Ven looked down at them speculatively.

"No," I said. "You have one, and that's enough."

"But," Ven said.

"I've humored you," I said. "I've let you act like a lower order. Now I want to see you behave like a civilized being. For unless you do, I shall have to take steps. I'm tired of this childishness."

"I'll be all right now," Ven replied. "We've come to an understanding." She gestured at Edith with her primary digit and the big mammal shivered. I wondered what Ven had done to her. Edith was thoroughly cowed—actually afraid of little Ven. Who was less than one-fifth her size. In a way, I felt an odd sort of pride in my mate that she should achieve mastery over such an intelligent and potentially dangerous brute. I knew perfectly well that I'd never dare attempt such dominance over Donald unless I was prepared to rob him of the mentality that made him useful. But I consoled myself with the thought that this female was peculiarly susceptible to domination.

"We'd better get that car out of sight," Ven said. She nodded to Edith. The human obediently trotted off in the direction of the car. A few moments later the sound of the motor rose and fell as she concealed it in the trees.

As soon as I could, I contacted Donald and told him what had happened. Fortunately he was alone, so his exclamation of surprise and consternation didn't arouse any suspicion.

"Ethanol, eh?" he said speculatively.

It was easy to follow the trend of his thoughts. "Don't get any ideas," I warned in my best TV villain manner. "I have Edith up here with me. If you want to see her again, you'd better stay sober."

"I wouldn't think of crossing you," he assured me insincerely. "I'm too close to being rid of you."

"Well—what do we do?" I asked. "You're the expert on this insane society of yours."

"You've done it," he said. "I don't think it was smart of you, but under the circumstances, I can't see how you could have done anything else. I warned you about Ven and Edith," he added—rather gloatingly, I thought. "Now you're in for it." His voice was almost gay.

"How?"

"Six women vanishing all at once is going to cause a stir even in Los Angeles," he said.

"After an ethanol party?" I asked curiously. "Six dancers out of a production that used a hundred? Your city will never miss them."

"But their families will."

Families! I hadn't thought of that. Mammals had strong family ties—probably due to their method of reproduction. We Thalassans, coming as we did from eggs, had none of this. The state incubators and the creches were our only contact with parenthood. We had no families. "Hmm," I said. "I hadn't thought of that."

"Well, you'd better start. I hope it gives you a headache."

"You get nastier every time I talk with you," I complained.

"I have my reasons," he said bitterly. "Now, if you're through with me, little master, I think I'd like to get some sleep. In the meantime you'd better get them back to their homes before they're missed."

"I can't," I confessed. "The controller isn't big enough to handle eight of you—not as individuals."

Donald chuckled grimly. "That's your worry. Remember, unless you find out which of them will be missed and act accordingly, you're going to be very much in the public eye."

I DIDN'T feel too happy as I cut off, but Donald had given me an idea.

One by one I checked the new proxies. Of the six, two were living together. They had the casual emotional involvement with males so characteristic of this species, but they could remain here for several days without causing comment. Of the re-remaining four, one had a roommate and would be difficult to extract; another was living alone; still another was mated and had an offspring, but she was not living with her mate—a legal action having separated her much as it separates incompatible Thalassans. The offspring, however, was living with her when she wasn't working, a not unusual situation on this world, but one that could have some complications unless she was returned to it very shortly.

The last was living with her parents and was seriously involved emotionally with a male. She was planning to be officially mated in the near future, although it would be legal fiction rather than fact since she was already nurturing a living embryo of some three weeks development. I debated whether to remove it, a simple enough manipulation, but decided against it. It would be interesting to observe a mammalian reproduction. But to remove her from her family and her unofficial mate was a task that might be difficult. I needed help.

I projected a call for Ven, phrasing it imperatively so she could have no doubt about its urgency. Her answer was quick and clear.

"I'm coming," she said.

"Good. I need you. And bring Edith. We have a problem that will require her talents."

"She'll be happy to cooperate." Ven's projection was cheerfully confident.

"You did her no permanent damage, I hope."

"Not a bit. In fact, you'd never know she's been disciplined."

"Well, get in here, both of you. We have work to do."

Edith had trouble squeezing into the control room and, despite her skin conditioning, the place quickly filled with her scent. But Ven and I were old hands now and took it in stride. She grasped the problem instantly. "The only one who might be any trouble is Alice. Her family and her boy friend can be difficult. The others won't need much effort, except for Grace. She'd better be returned to her baby as soon as possible."

"How soon?" I asked.

"The baby isn't living with her," Edith added, "not while she's working, but she sees it regularly. Every day or two, I believe."

I sighed. That solved the biggest problem.

"We had better start at once," Ven said.

I IGNORED her and looked inquiringly at Edith. "What would you do?" I asked, flashing a cold projection at Ven to stay out of this.

"Well—if I had to do it, I'd send Alice and Grace home. I wouldn't do anything to Alice except block her from talking about this place and what happened. Grace I'd put under full control, have her pick up her baby, go home, and pack to leave. As soon as she's ready to go, bring her out here."

"The infant, too?"

"Of course. A baby's no bother."

This, I thought, was something of an understatement.

"And what of the others?" I asked.

"Velma has a nosey roommate. Have her start a fight and leave angry. She hasn't much baggage, and it won't be any trouble for her to collect it. As for the other three, I think Joan's being kept. She can't afford a single apartment on her salary. Loleta and Marian are always out, sometimes for days. Their landlady won't think a thing of it. If they never return, she'll just pack their things and rent the room to someone else. I know that old witch. I'd just keep those three here and not worry about them. Nobody's going to make any fuss about three chorines disappearing. Later on you can make them write letters enclosing money to send their clothes to another city. Then they can be picked up and stored. That should give us a year before anyone gets suspicious enough to look for them."

"Edith," I said, "you're a genius."

"I got you into this mess," Edith said. "So, perhaps I'd better get you out."

"But your fellow mammals—"

"You haven't hurt me—not much, anyway," Edith said. "So I don't suppose you'll hurt them. And, besides, I don't want Ven mad at me like she was this afternoon. Anyway—you'll be gone soon."

"I think I shall regret leaving," I said honestly. "There is a great deal about you mammals I am beginning to suspect I do not know."

"You aren't kidding," she said with faint bitterness so similar to Donald's that my antennae quivered. "But it's been quite an experience. I'll tell my kids when I have them—but they're not going to believe me."

"I hope you have those children and raise them to maturity," I said.

The tone of my voice caused her to look at me with sudden fear on her face. But at the sight of my impassive features it died away. "You scared me for a moment," she said.

"Did I? I didn't mean to."

CHAPTER SEVEN

THE next week kept us busy following Edith's instructions. I didn't see how they would apply to Alice, but Edith knew her species better than I. Alice's silence and the prying inquisitiveness of her parents and her boyfriend worked like magic. Alice finally became angry and after a stormy scene left the house, swearing never to return. Edith picked her up as she walked away; Ven turned on the control and turned the threat to fact. Later I took a leaf from Edith's book and sent Alice to San Francisco, where I had her write a pair of bitter letters to her parents and her extralegal mate. After that I felt more secure.

The others worked out exactly as Edith predicted. No trouble at all. By the time Donald returned from the East with a ton of tin ingots in a small truck our training schedule was well set up. The robots and I had managed to build a multiplex controller similar to those we used on Thalassa on the state farms, but much smaller. It could handle the proxies en masse or as individuals. While far less sensitive than the one in the ship, it was effective enough for our rather elementary purposes.

Edith, who was running the group under Ven's supervision, had them lined up in a row to greet Donald as he came up the hill toward the ship.

"The place looks like a nudist colony," Donald grumbled. "You haven't improved it any." He eyed the file of mammals trooping down to the truck to unload the tin ingots. "I have another ton lined up for delivery as soon as you get this processed," he said.

"Good," I replied. "We'll leave as soon as it's aboard. I don't like the looks of your recent actions."

"Mine?" I shook my head. "Oh, you mean the world situation." I nodded. "You shouldn't worry about it. You should have seen it this time last year."

I shrugged. I would never really understand these creatures. Their brains functioned differently. "You frighten me with your wild displays of emotion. Someday one of you is going to start something and your world is going to go up in fire."

"I don't think so," he said. "I have some ideas about that. With the money from your stories and with what you have taught me, I think there will be some changes." There was a peculiar expression in his eyes that I couldn't identify. It made me vaguely uneasy. "I've been doing a lot of thinking since you met up with Edie and me. What this world needs is someone who can run it."

"That's obvious," I said. "Until your society catches up with your technology you will be in constant danger. You mammals will have to learn to discipline your emotions."

His face twisted. "I've had a good practical course in that," he said. "Now I'm getting postgraduate training." He gestured at the women coming up the hill carrying the silver tin ingots. "Just how long do you think I can endure something like this?"

"Like what?" I asked.

"Do I have to draw you a diagram?" he asked. "Ever since you lizards came into my life I haven't been able to touch a woman. Not even Edith—and she's my wife. Just how much of this do you think I can take?"

"OH!" I exclaimed with dawning comprehension. "I think I see."

The situation would have been amusing if it wasn't so stupid. I was surprised that I hadn't realized it before. There was, I knew, a certain amount of feedback in a bipolar control circuit. Obviously enough of Ven's conditioning, and mine, had seeped through to affect Donald and Edith's normal relationships. Mammals were far more preoccupied with sex than we were. Their books, magazines, television, and motion pictures reeked of it. It was present in almost every piece of advertising, and four of our six new proxies were living histories of it. Yet Donald and Edith, because of our feedback, had been kept as continent as novitiates for the priesthood of Authority!

"I'm a perfectly normal male," Donald said. "Just what do you think you've been doing to me? I can't drink. I can't make love. I can't do anything except collect tin for you lizards. Just why do you think I hate you? Now you surround me with a whole damned untouchable harem! Are you trying to drive me insane?"

I laughed, and Donald recognized the sound for what it was.

"Oh, *damn* you!" he said bitterly. "How would you like to be married for eight months and for six of them be unable to touch your wife? Just why do you think Edith tried to get drunk? I could kill you cheerfully for what you've done to us!"

"Oh!" I said. There was a world of understanding opening in front of me. Of course, it would do no good to tell him that Ven and I had remained in enforced continence for five years. It was just the Eugenics council working through us—entirely involuntarily. What was bothering Donald and Edith was so absurdly simple that neither Ven nor I would have thought to ask. And the mammals with their peculiar customs and habits would never have told us unless—as had happened—the pressure became too great.

What our mammals needed was a good dose of Va Krul's basic therapy. If Edith were fertilized as a result of it, so much the better. It would keep her attention where it more properly belonged. The thought would never have occurred to me in my present state. Since I was content, I had erroneously assumed that everything was in harmony.

"You might as well go home," I said. "Take Edith with you. We won't need you for several days."

"Why?"

"You'll find things a little different. I'll make a few adjustments on the controller."

TO my surprise Don didn't appear happy at all. "Does that mean what I think it does?" he demanded. "Do you think I'll get any satisfaction out of being controlled even *there?*"

"I don't know about the pleasure," I said coldly, "but I do know that it will improve your attitude."

Donald raged at me, his brain white with anger. "So help me God, Eu Kor, someday I'm going to kill you for this! It's the ultimate insult."

"You're not going to do anything," I said calmly. His voice dissolved into obscenity. For a moment I felt sorry for him until I remembered the basic truth that none of us are free—and the most intelligent, naturally, are the least free of all. They are bound by their commitments, their duties, their responsibilities, and by their intelligence itself. If a superior intelligence occasionally exhibits petty lapses—which amuse him or relieve his boredom—it is not the place of the less endowed to construe it as a sign of equality.

Some—like Ven and me—have known their place from birth. Others, like Edith and Alice, learn easily with a minimum amount of pain. Some like Grace learn hard; and some—like Donald—do not learn at all.

Donald was the eternal rebel, complying because he must, yet seething with resentment because he did. He was the personification of drive without innate control, ambition without humility, intelligence without wisdom. As he had been, he was not quite enough. At best he would have been a minor author and a petty domestic tyrant. He would never have been a threat simply because he didn't have the ability or training. But I had given him what he lacked. The knowledge I had impressed upon his mind would give him a tremendous advantage over his fellow mammals, and his tendencies toward domestic tyranny would expand to include others. His glandular attitude would pervert his knowledge to the detriment of humankind. He could become a thing so dangerous that it could destroy this precariously balanced world.

I went into the ship and set up a world matrix on the computer, using all the data I had accumulated, secured the answer, and then inserted Donald's potential into the matrix. I then ordered a probability extrapolation for both matrices, equating the solutions with survival.

The answers confirmed my thoughts. With the matrix as it stood, the twenty-year survival prediction was 65 per cent, which wasn't too bad since few advanced-technology worlds have better than an 85 per cent survival probability. But with Donald in the matrix, the survival prediction was zero!

I knew what I must do. I could not leave him behind as I had planned. Nor could I inflict the senseless cruelty of brainblotting. He would have to be mercifully destroyed.

Although I was fond of Donald, and his death would leave me sick for weeks, it would not be right to let my creation live and condemn the mammal race to death. I could not exterminate a race Authority had created. The guilt syndrome would be shattering. Of course, if they killed each other that was not my concern.

But until we left I would give him all the freedom he could use. Outside of the minimum of control, he would be free to do and act as he pleased. I didn't owe it to him, yet it was not his fault that he had come into my hands. And when I returned to Thalassa I would tell the Council what I had done and ask for justice. Perhaps we could save this world from itself even as we had saved others. The question of gratitude would be immaterial.

With a firm hand to set them on the track, the mammals might learn the values of intelligence and cooperation before it was too late. They might understand the realities of existence rather than fall victim to their glandular fancies. They might. But if they did, one thing would be certain— they would learn it the hard way. Donald was proof of that.

I went to our living quarters, and presently Ven joined me. "They're all in for the night, Eu," she said.

"That's good. How are they coming along?"

"Splendidly. Another week should see the end of the training. Edith was a good experience for me in handling these. I'm not making the mistakes I did. I'm finding the blocks and removing them. One of them, the one called Grace, should be even better than Edith."

"As a mount?" I asked with faint humor. "Or as a working proxy?"

"Both," Ven said promptly. "She's stronger and more intelligent. Yet even so I think I shall always like Edith best."

"ONE'S first dependent is always one's fondest memory," I replied sententiously. "But you'll forget them all when we're back on Thalassa."

"I won't," Ven said. "I'll never forget Edith."

"Never is a long time," I said gently. "I shall even forget the pain of killing Donald some day."

"Then you've decided to eliminate him?" Ven said.

I nodded. "It's necessary," I said. "This world wouldn't be safe with him alive."

"Poor Edith. She's fond of the brute," Ven said. She moved toward the doorway.

"Where are you going?" I asked.

"I want to talk to Edith. Perhaps I can prepare her."

"No. Don't," I said. "Contact her if you wish, but tell her nothing."

"Very well," she said. I smiled as she disappeared. Ven was going to miss her pet once we had left. It was obvious.

"Eu! Quick!" Ven's projection crackled in my brain. "They're fighting! Edith's being hurt, and I can't touch them! They've set up a block!"

I ran for the control room, slapped the helmet on my head, reached for the controls—and stopped, laughing.

"Stop them!" Ven screamed. Her aura blazed a brilliant white and her projection nearly knocked me down. She reached for the control switch, but I slapped her hand away.

"Quiet!" I snapped. "They're not fighting, you little fool! Turn on your audio and listen and stop acting silly!"

Ven did as I told her and her aura changed to a fiery pink. "Oh!" she said in a small voice, "but they never—"

I must have made some mistake in revising the controllers—or feedback was stronger than I suspected—for the Va Krul syndrome came back along our lines of contact with explosive force! Desperately I reached for the switch—but my hand froze in midair as an intolerable wave of emotion drove Ven and me together like two pieces of iron with opposite magnetic charge! The last thing I remember was being enveloped in the flaring golden glow of Ven's aura.

I CAME to my senses in our living quarters. I was stunned—exhausted—limp and gasping.

"Thalassa!" I said weakly, "we've *really* done it now!"

Ven smiled a pale blue radiance at me. "You have become strong, living on this heavy world," she said. "I like it."

"But—but!" I sputtered. "It was so—it can't—it couldn't—"

"But it did," Ven said softly. "And I'm glad it did."

"I don't mean that. What I mean to say was that it was so—"

"Unexpected?"

"No! So utterly—"

"Satisfying?" she asked.

"Stop interrupting! It was all of that and more. But what I want to say is that we've violated the prime restriction for space travelers. How could we do it?"

"You're forgetting that for some time we have been living upon this emotion-charged world," Ven said. "The steady erosion was more than our conditioning could take. The feedback was merely the last in a whole series of disruptive stimuli. It was the trigger, but our defenses had been weakened long before. Not that I'm sorry," she added quickly. "For weeks I've been wondering what sort of a mate you'd be when this trip was over. I'm not unhappy with the preview." She smiled at me and the whole of our living quarters was filled with a bright tender blue.

"The natives," I said worriedly. "We were in contact with them."

Ven's aura darkened. "I had forgotten them," she said. "I hope that the feedback wasn't intensified and returned to them. I'd better look." She started for the control room and I followed more slowly.

"There's no damage," she said from beneath the helmet. "Edith feels just as I do."

I took my helmet and coded Don's pattern on the selector. Peculiar, I thought with vague wonder. Most peculiar. For the first time Donald and I were in true rapport. His mind was slow, lazy, sluggish—even his ambition was sated for the moment. Could it be, I wondered, that we could find agreement through our emotions? Was it frustration that drove him? Whatever the block had been it was gone now. This was a true empathic meeting—something far more satisfying than our previous conflict.

I relaxed in it, feeling the slow langorous questings of his mind even as he felt mine. There was a sense of brotherhood that transcended differences in race and culture. We were down to basics, on the oldest meeting ground of life.

He was wondering idly what the outcome of this might be—conscious of me, but careless. It jolted me. He might be uncertain, but I *knew* Ven was from good family stock, and "good" to a Thalassan meant something entirely different than it commonly did to the natives of this planet!

I disengaged hurriedly and shook Ven out of her rapport with Edith. "We've no time to lose," I said. "We must leave at once! You know what's going to happen!"

"I know," Ven said. "I feel the changes already."

"That's just in your mind," I snapped.

"We're not going home," she said. There was a note of prophecy in her voice. "We'll never make it."

"We can't stay here!"

"I know."

"Then what are we going to do?"

WE couldn't stay here. But we couldn't go home either. The trip would take weeks, and hyperspace is fatal to a gravid Thalassan female. That was something we learned long ago, and the principal reason for continence-conditioning for couples in space. What was more, I knew that where Ven stayed, I would stay.

"Remember the fourth planet of this system?" Ven asked.

"Yes. Ideal gravity, adequate oxygen, but too cold."

"And with no intelligent life," Ven added. "That's an advantage—and we can beat the cold. It wouldn't be too hard to build domes. We have plenty of power metal, and a matricizer. We could hatch our clutch there. With the mammals to help us, we should be able to make a comfortable enough life for the forty years it'll take to bring our offspring to maturity. We should be able to do this easily, and still get home before we're strangers."

"Hmm," I said. "It's possible. And we can use this world for a supply base. But would you care to live on that cold barren planet?"

"There are worse places," she said matter-of-factly. "And we'd be close to everything we'd need."

It did have possibilities. And the mammals could be adapted. They were a more advanced evolutionary form than we, but lower on the adaptive scale—nonspecialized—more so than any other intelligent race I had encountered.

Ven said, "We would actually be doing their race a favor, if the computation of this world's future is correct. Some of them would still survive if this planet commits suicide. And if the prediction is wrong, we would have done no harm. If they reach space, they'll merely find that they've already arrived when they reach the fourth planet."

"Which might be something of a surprise to their explorers," I said with a chuckle. "All right. We'll play it your way."

I was pretty sure how Donald would take this. He was going to be furious, but after all one doesn't make a pet of a wolf and then turn it loose. It's too hard on the livestock. But I didn't think he'd be too unhappy. He'd be the principal human on Mars; and after we left he'd be ruler of a world. And in the meantime he could be a domestic tyrant.

It was fortunate, I thought with a smile, that mammals were essentially polygamous. Donald would make some nasty comments about being a herd sire—but I didn't think his comments would be too sincere. After all, it's not every man that has a chance to become a founding father.

I was still smiling as I turned the dials on the controller and flipped the switch. Founding father—the title was as much mine as his!

THE END

If you've enjoyed this book, you will not want to miss these terrific titles…

ARMCHAIR SCI-FI & HORROR DOUBLE NOVELS, $12.95 each

D-1 **THE GALAXY RAIDERS** by William P. McGivern
SPACE STATION #1 by Frank Belknap Long

D-2 **THE PROGRAMMED PEOPLE** by Jack Sharkey
SLAVES OF THE CRYSTAL BRAIN by William Carter Sawtelle

D-3 **YOU'RE ALL ALONE** by Fritz Leiber
THE LIQUID MAN by Bernard C. Gilford

D-4 **CITADEL OF THE STAR LORDS** by Edmond Hamilton
VOYAGE TO ETERNITY by Milton Lesser

D-5 **IRON MEN OF VENUS** by Don Wilcox
THE MAN WITH ABSOLUTE MOTION by Noel Loomis

D-6 **WHO SOWS THE WIND…** by Rog Phillips
THE PUZZLE PLANET by Robert A. W. Lowndes

D-7 **PLANET OF DREAD** by Murray Leinster
TWICE UPON A TIME by Charles L. Fontenay

D-8 **THE TERROR OUT OF SPACE** by Dwight V. Swain
QUEST OF THE GOLDEN APE by Ivar Jorgensen and Adam Chase

D-9 **SECRET OF MARRACOTT DEEP** by Henry Slesar
PAWN OF THE BLACK FLEET by Mark Clifton.

D-10 **BEYOND THE RINGS OF SATURN** by Robert Moore Williams
A MAN OBSESSED by Alan E. Nourse

ARMCHAIR SCIENCE FICTION CLASSICS, $12.95 each

C-1 **THE GREEN MAN**
by Harold M. Sherman

C-2 **A TRACE OF MEMORY**
By Keith Laumer

C-3 **INTO PLUTONIAN DEPTHS**
by Stanton A. Coblentz

ARMCHAIR MASTERS OF SCIENCE FICTION SERIES, $16.95 each

M-1 **MASTERS OF SCIENCE FICTION, Vol. One**
Bryce Walton—"Dark of the Moon" and other tales

M-2 **MASTERS OF SCIENCE FICTION, Vol. Two**
Jerome Bixby—"One Way Street" and other tales

If you've enjoyed this book, you will not want to miss these terrific titles…

ARMCHAIR SCI-FI & HORROR DOUBLE NOVELS, $12.95 each

D-11 **PERIL OF THE STARMEN** by Kris Neville
THE STRANGE INVASION by Murray Leinster

D-12 **THE STAR LORD** by Boyd Ellanby
CAPTIVES OF THE FLAME by Samuel R. Delany

D-13 **MEN OF THE MORNING STAR** by Edmond Hamilton
PLANET FOR PLUNDER by Hal Clement and Sam Merwin, Jr.

D-14 **ICE CITY OF THE GORGON** by Chester S. Geier and Richard Shaver
WHEN THE WORLD TOTTERED by Lester del Rey

D-15 **WORLDS WITHOUT END** by Clifford D. Simak
THE LAVENDER VINE OF DEATH by Don Wilcox

D-16 **SHADOW ON THE MOON** by Joe Gibson
ARMAGEDDON EARTH by Geoff St. Reynard

D-17 **THE GIRL WHO LOVED DEATH** by Paul W. Fairman
SLAVE PLANET by Laurence M. Janifer

D-18 **SECOND CHANCE** by J. F. Bone
MISSION TO A DISTANT STAR by Frank Belknap Long

D-19 **THE SYNDIC** by C. M. Kornbluth
FLIGHT TO FOREVER by Poul Anderson

D-20 **SOMEWHERE I'LL FIND YOU** by Milton Lesser
THE TIME ARMADA by Fox B. Holden

ARMCHAIR SCIENCE FICTION CLASSICS, $12.95 each

C-4 **CORPUS EARTHLING**
by Louis Charbonneau

C-5 **THE TIME DISSOLVER**
by Jerry Sohl

C-6 **WEST OF THE SUN**
by Edgar Pangborn

ARMCHAIR SCI-FI & HORROR GEMS SERIES, $12.95 each

G-1 **SCIENCE FICTION GEMS, Vol. One**
Isaac Asimov and others

G-2 **HORROR GEMS, Vol. One**
Carl Jacobi and others

If you've enjoyed this book, you will not want to miss these terrific titles...

ARMCHAIR SCI-FI & HORROR DOUBLE NOVELS, $12.95 each

If you've enjoyed this book, you will not want to miss these terrific titles...

If you've enjoyed this book, you will not want to miss these terrific titles…

If you've enjoyed this book, you will not want to miss these terrific titles…

ARMCHAIR SCI-FI & HORROR DOUBLE NOVELS, $12.95 each

D-141 **ALL HEROES ARE HATED** by Milton Lesser
AND THE STARS REMAIN by Bryan Berry

D-142 **LAST CALL FOR DOOMSDAY** by Edmond Hamilton
HUNTRESS OF AKKAN by Robert Moore Williams

D-143 **THE MOON PIRATES** by Neil R. Jones
CALLISTO AT WAR by Harl Vincent

D-144 **THUNDER IN THE DAWN** by Henry Kuttner
THE UNCANNY EXPERIMENTS OF DR. VARSAG by David V. Reed

D-145 **A PATTERN FOR MONSTERS** by Randall Garrett
STAR SURGEON by Alan E Nourse

D-146 **THE ATOM CURTAIN** by Nick Boddie Williams
WARLOCK OF SHARRADOR by Gardner F. Fox

D-147 **SECRET OF THE LOST PLANET** by David Wright O'Brien
TELEVISION HILL by George McLociard

D-148 **INTO THE GREEN PRISM** by A Hyatt Verrill
WANDERERS OF THE WOLF-MOON by Nelson S. Bond

D-149 **MINIONS OF THE TIGER** by Chester S. Geier
FOUNDING FATHER by J. F. Bone

D-150 **THE INVISIBLE MAN** by H. G. Wells
THE ISLAND OF DR. MOREAU by H. G. Wells

ARMCHAIR SCIENCE FICTION CLASSICS, $12.95 each

C-61 **THE SHAVER MYSTERY, Book Six**
by Richard. S. Shaver

C-62 **CADUCEUS WILD**
by Ward Moore & Robert Bradford

ARMCHAIR MYSTERY-CRIME DOUBLE NOVELS, $12.95 each

B-1 **THE DEADLY PICK-UP** by Milton Ozaki
KILLER TAKE ALL by James O. Causey

B-2 **THE VIOLENT ONES** by E. Howard Hunt
HIGH HEEL HOMICIDE by Frederick C. Davis

B-3 **FURY ON SUNDAY** by Richard Matheson
THE AGONY COLUMN by Earl Derr Biggers